P9-BYV-400

DEAR RACHEL MADDOW

DEAR RACHEL MADDOW

A NOVEL

ADRIENNE KISNER

FEIWEL AND FRIENDS

NEW YORK

A FEIWEL AND FRIENDS BOOK
An imprint of Macmillan Publishing Group, LLC
175 Fifth Avenue, New York, NY 10010

Our books may be purchased in bulk for promotional, educational, or business use. Please
contact your local bookseller or the Macmillan Corporate and Premium Sales Department at
(800) 221-7945 ext. 5442 or by e-mail at MacmillanSpecialMarkets@macmillan.com.

Library of Congress Cataloging-in-Publication Data is available.

ISBN 978-1-250-14602-1 (hardcover) / ISBN 978-1-250-14601-4 (ebook)

Book design by Rebecca Syracuse

Feiwel and Friends logo designed by Filomena Tuosto

First edition, 2018

1 3 5 7 9 10 8 6 4 2

fiercereads.com

TO NA, AMANDA, AND AMY—
WITH ALL MY HEART

Folder: Sent
To: Egrimm@westing.pa.edu
From: Brynnieh0401@gmail.com
Date: September 10
Subject: School Assignment

Dear Rachel Maddow,

I am writing to you because of a school assignment. It's a totally ridiculous reason to be writing, but I don't think you'll actually read it anyway. This kind of thing is so sixth grade. I am a junior in high school and I've been forced to write to a "celebrity hero" by the Applied English teacher. (Hey, Mr. Grimm! How's it hanging, buddy?) I wasn't going to do it, because my ex-girlfriend worships you and, hello, school assignment. But I turned on your show and Mom totally freaked out to see me watching you. Apparently your *liberal* and *leftist* views don't sit well with her. Mom spat out the words like she was talking about my dad, so I knew she meant it. That made you my celebrity hero.

You were talking about some guys running for Congress. But then you said one of them was "freaking amazing." I don't think newspeople are supposed to say things like that. And isn't that biased? Newspeople aren't supposed to be biased. I know this because Mr. Grimm made us watch this video about newswriting. Though no one else knows this about me, Rachel Maddow, I have a near photographic memory for stuff people say. Their words just stick in my brain. So I remember what a reporter is *supposed* to do.

Anyway, thanks for pissing off my mom.

Sincerely,
Brynn Harper

Folder:	Inbox
To:	Brynnieh0401@gmail.com
From:	Egrimm@westing.pa.edu
Date:	September 11
Subject:	RE: School Assignment

Dear Rachel Maddow,

I am writing to you because of a school assignment. ~~It's a totally ridiculous reason to be writing, but I don't think you actually read it anyway. This kind of thing is so sixth grade.~~ [Brynn, this is good, honest writing. Can you try to put a positive spin on it?] I am a junior in high school and I've been ~~forced~~ asked to write to a "celebrity hero" by the Applied English teacher. ~~(Hey, Mr. Grimm! How's it hanging, buddy?)~~ [I'm doing well, thanks. But you can take this out.] ~~I wasn't going to do it, because my ex-girlfriend worships you and, hello, school assignment.~~ But I turned on your show and Mom totally freaked out to see me watching you. Apparently your *liberal* and *leftist* views still don't sit well with her. Mom spat out the words like she was talking about my dad, so I knew she meant it. That made you my celebrity hero. [Again, great personal touch. But maybe too intimate for this correspondence?]

You were talking about some guys running for Congress. But then you said one of them was "freaking amazing." And I don't think newspeople are supposed to say things like that. And isn't that biased? Newspeople aren't supposed to be biased. I know this because Mr. Grimm, my Applied English teacher, made us watch this video about newswriting. Though no one else knows this about me, Rachel Maddow, I have a photographic memory for stuff people say. Their words just stick in my brain. So I remember what a reporter is *supposed* to do. [You are right, Brynn! I didn't know that about you. Shouldn't you remember your assignments, then?]

~~Anyway, thanks for pissing off my mom.~~ [There is a list of questions I asked you to include. Maybe you could end with that instead.]

Sincerely,

Brynn Harper

Folder:	Sent
To:	Egrimm@westing.pa.edu
Cc:	Rachel@msnbc.com
From:	Brynnieh0401@gmail.com
Date:	September 12
Subject:	School Assignment Again

Dear Rachel Maddow,

I learned an important lesson about rough drafts. If you really want to send someone a letter, you should just send it. Do *not* turn it in to your English teacher first. But Mr. Grimm (said English teacher) is the only person I know who doesn't think I'm hopeless, so I am trying this again for his sake. Though I'm sending it to you, too, to *avoid further editing*.

My name is Brynn Harper and I am sixteen years old. I live with my mother and stepfather in Westing, Pennsylvania. I have a brother, too. Or, I had one, anyway.

I first watched your show a couple of times freshman year because my best friend (well, okay, my girlfriend) loved you, so she kind of dragged me along with her. She's not my girlfriend anymore. And she said she didn't have time to watch television anymore, either, even for you. So she dumped us both. That gives us something in common.

I had a list of questions that I was supposed to ask you, but I got most of the answers online already. Mr. Grimm suggested I think of new ones. So here you go:

> 1. When you look at the papers on your desk and circle something, are you really reading from them? Don't you read from a teleprompter? When you go to commercial, you shuffle those papers, too. Seriously, is there anything even written on them?
>
> 2. How much does a person have to know to be considered a "wonk"?

3

3. At least one person laughs in the background while you are talking. Is this on purpose? Who is that?

4. Why don't you run for political office?

5. Is there ever a staff meeting when you think to yourself, "Huh, there really *isn't* a lot going on in the news today"?

6. How many pairs of shoes do you actually own?

Sincerely,

Brynn Harper

Folder: Sent
To: Rachel@msnbc.com
From: Brynnieh0401@gmail.com
Date: September 14
Subject: Jumping for joy

Dear Rachel Maddow,

I am embarrassed to say that I literally squealed in the library when I got your e-mail. I scared the hell out of one of the librarians. She came over to yell at me, and I just sort of jabbed at the computer screen and jumped up and down in my seat. When she figured out that you had written back to me, she just grinned and gave me a thumbs-up.

I made the mistake of forwarding your e-mail to Mr. Grimm. He said I had to answer back *again*. I was so disgusted with the idea that a good thing would lead to *more work* that I complained about it at home. Mom went nuts. I sort of lied and told her I was *assigned* to write to you (which, technically, was true). She and my stepdad (aka the Fart Weasel, a name I gave him years ago that stuck in my head because even his whiskers smell like fart) then went on an angry rant about bombast and lies and liberals and blah blah blah. The Fart Weasel said he'd even talk to Mr. Grimm on my behalf, which I knew would never happen, because that would require him to make an actual effort in this life. But their reaction sealed my fate. Obviously I would write back to you.

Your fan,
Brynn Harper

Folder:	Inbox
To:	Brynnieh0401@gmail.com
From:	Egrimm@westing.pa.edu
Date:	September 17
Subject:	RE: The Blues

Dear Rachel Maddow,

Mr. Grimm has used the fact that you wrote back to me after our hero assignment to discuss "cause and effect." ~~This might seem pretty basic for a junior English class, but be*cause* I gave up on being Brynn the Scholar a while ago, the *effect* is that I am in the basement of the school, where the rooms don't have numbers, only colors.~~ [Brynn—I don't mind if you retain the epistolary format for assignments, if this is what inspires you to do your work. However, keep in mind that if you intend to send this, you might want to be a little less confessional and a little more formal.] Us "Applied" juniors are in the blue room (as opposed to the Honors/AP or Academic students allowed to walk in the sun aboveground). I started freshman year on the Honors track, but was shuffled into Academic shortly into my sophomore year. By the end of it, my mom said I was going to end up like my brother and I had better get my act together. My journalism teacher referred me for a shit ton of assessments, which got me into Applied, where I could get "more attention." I thought all I needed was to give more of a shit, but it turns out speech-to-text technology makes me a writing fiend. (Note: I still actually need to give more of a shit.) We have three teachers who teach us in shifts along with the ninth, tenth, and twelfth graders. They always look tired, even with near constant caffeination. [Good use of imagery, but let us both agree never to share this with the rest of your faculty.] Passing junior and senior year in the Applied Color Room Kingdom is Brynnie's Last Chance at graduating, because the numbered rooms of tiny Westing High gave up on the Brynnster for good last May.

The blue room crew is cool. The best of us is Lacey, who chills in her wheelchair using her voice board to communicate. She is quick with that thing, and her brain works about a thousand times faster than mine. She is actually an Honors/AP senior, though I don't hold that against her. Since she's the smartest person ever, the school lets her do basically whatever she wants. She gets bored with high school classes and even the extra community college classes she takes. Thus she spends a lot of time with us as a "resident peer tutor." This works out for me because she's super-nice and has kind of taken me on as a special project. Greg, Lance, Riley, Bianca, and I (the Applied junior crew) basically see Lacey as another teacher.

Do you get lost effects from lost causes? I'll have to ask Mr. Grimm. I think he'd be happy to learn I was paying attention to the lesson. [You know . . . I actually am. Though none of you are lost causes. Please consider adding a few more paragraphs addressing the specifics of this assignment, "Cause and Effect in My Daily Life."]

Sincerely,
Brynn

Folder:	Drafts
To:	Rachel@msnbc.com
From:	Brynnieh0401@gmail.com
Date:	September 18
Subject:	Got the blues

Dear Rachel Maddow,

I had a pen pal once in fifth grade. I loved writing to her, even if I hated the physical act of writing. It felt good to put all my words some place. So, I'll keep writing to you. Don't tell Mr. Grimm. If he knew I was doing it so much on my own, it might go to his head.

Today, to suck as much as humanly possible out of something interesting, Mr. Grimm put us in pairs to talk about our hero assignments. Peer Mentor Lacey was stuck with me. She did the assignment just for fun even though she didn't have to.

"So, that's the lady with the one eyebrow?" I said of her hero.

"Yes." Lacey sighed. She did that a lot with me. "But she painted herself as she was, see. . . ."

"But she's dead. You wrote to a dead person?"

"I interpreted the assignment. She is famous. She is my hero. Like Grimm would argue with me. I'm not even a student in this class."

"Well played." I whistled. I was mostly annoyed that I didn't think of something like that.

"And you like a pundit. Fascinating."

"She is a scholar and a storyteller," I said, bowing my head reverently and putting my hand on my heart. "Politics are her canvas."

Lacey chuckled. "Well. We both like artists, then."

"Yes."

"Did you know that Frida Kahlo was also in a wheelchair?" Lacey said.

"No. I don't think I did. Did you know that Rachel was the first out Rhodes Scholar?"

"Yes."

"Of course you did," I said. "You know everything."

"Not everything."

"Seems like it." I crossed my arms. "Are you sure you don't want to go out with me?"

"I had to agree not to date my mentees. You and I have had this discussion. Also, I'm still into guys."

"Fine. That makes no sense to me. But fine."

Lacey laughed. Her laugh sounds a little like wind chimes.

Sincerely,

Brynn

Folder: Drafts
To: Rachel@msnbc.com
From: Brynnieh0401@gmail.com
Date: September 19
Subject: Journalism

Dear Rachel Maddow,

Confession: I used to be on the school paper. That's actually how I really got to know my ex-girlfriend Sarah. One day in ninth grade I was pulled out of study hall and taken to a room far in the north wing. It was way sketch but when I got there, I wasn't bound and gagged. Instead, I met Mr. McCloud, journalism teacher extraordinaire.

"Ms. Harper. I'm told you have a way with words," he said.

"I do? By who?"

Mr. McCloud smirked. "By whom. But that wouldn't have rhymed."

I shrugged.

As it turned out, that was the start of Brynn the Investigative Beat Reporter. I didn't investigate so much as write little articles about the sports ball players or about the 4-H kids' winning rabbits or about the events at the War Memorial downtown. But I loved it, especially my War Memorial beat. Every stupid little slice of life piece I wrote. It's fitting that the War Memorial practically burned down in August. The causes are still under investigation and have been deemed suspicious. You can still overhear kids talking about it in the halls at least once a week.

If I had the grades, I'd be reporting the fuck out of that.

Especially because firecrackers had been found at the scene.

And because the story seemed to die out on television and print and even online. That had to mean something, didn't it?

And because people are still interested. The War Memorial was a big deal in town.

Is someone trying to cover up something? Who? What?

First I had to crack the case of a 2.3 GPA to get back on the paper. Then I could run wild with my conspiracy theories for fun and credit.

You used to be on the radio. You said you loved it, too. I get it. There's something so satisfying about telling people stories.

About telling people's *stories*.

But at the end of last year, my grades weren't high enough to stay with the paper. I don't know why that matters. I can still write, you know? But the guidance counselor said I had to "focus on academics." Maybe losing the paper would "motivate" me to "improve" and "rejoin later."

I miss the fucking school paper with all the shards of my shattered heart. I miss its online edition with the hideous layout. I miss all twenty of our bimonthly subscribers (not counting the staff) and their inane comments on every article. I loved every stupid word anyone wrote. I loved it and then I lost it.

This has not motivated me. Loss isn't motivating. It's debilitating.

I don't have Sarah anymore. I don't have the paper.

I guess I only have you.

Sincerely,

Brynn

Folder:	Drafts
To:	Rachel@msnbc.com
From:	Brynnieh0401@gmail.com
Date:	September 20
Subject:	Justin Time

Dear Rachel Maddow,

I stand corrected. I have you and a kid named Justin.

One of the chief characteristics of a good reporter, you may agree, is persistence. Justin Mitchell, ace investigator for the *Westing High Gazette*, is the freckled embodiment of persistence.

Today I walked to my classroom, wondering if I should take the long route past Sarah's locker, when Justin stopped me.

"Well, hello," he said.

"Hey," I said.

"How are you? Are you coming back to the paper? We need you. Things are getting weird. I can't even tell you how weird, because it's kind of a secret? But if you were there, you would know and then we could talk about it. How are your grades? Are they up yet? I guess not because we've only had a few weeks of school, but maybe I could help you and, oh man, maybe you could just do a column or something with a pen name."

This is how Justin talks.

"I can't, in fact, come back to the paper. Summer school didn't go so great."

"Maybe I could talk to someone."

"Good luck with that," I said.

"Listen, Brynn. This sucks. It all sucks. But don't be a stranger? Okay? I'm around."

"Okay, sure, Justin."

"I'm serious." Justin seemed to be staring at something over my shoulder. His freckles were kind of melting together.

"Are you blushing?" I asked. I turned and saw Lacey was in the elevator. I looked back at Justin.

"Shut up. I'll talk to you later." He turned and abruptly walked away.

"Lacey, my friend," I said, sticking myself in between the closing elevator doors. "I don't suppose you want to take my quiz for me. I have one for Ms. Yee in about five minutes."

"Sure, Brynn. I'm positive no one will notice me doing that, and of course I don't care if your teachers can tell whether you learned the material or not."

"You and your stupid ethics," I said. The elevator door slid open.

I emerged unto my basement kingdom, away from the one that used to be mine. Lacey made me go in the classroom first just to be sure I didn't try to make a break for it away from the quiz at the last second.

Sincerely,

Brynn

Folder: Drafts
To: Rachel@msnbc.com
From: Brynnieh0401@gmail.com
Date: September 21
Subject: Oh Brother, Where Art Thou?

Dear Rachel Maddow,

You have a brother. Is he nice?

My brother was nice. When I was twelve, he got me a pair of ice skates for my birthday. I resented it because I felt too old for that sort of thing, but they were from Nick so I pretended to love them. The War Memorial used to host ice-skating every other weekend. It still would have, probably, if half of it wasn't charred rubble from the fire. Earlier today Justin had showed me a clipping from the *Tribune* that investigators still weren't releasing further information. That was still weird as fuck.

Mostly people went there to get stoned in the bushes, but I didn't know what that was back then. Nick had just gotten his license and drove us to the rink. It was filled with hockey dudes and their girlfriends. Nick was cool with everyone then, just this big guy with a too-big laugh and too-big sense of humor. He held me up and dragged me around and around the rink until I finally started to be able to balance on my own. When I finally made it around without falling, Nick bought me a slice of pizza. We sat at the long counter, and I watched couples skate—the girls backward, the boys guiding them around while trying to sneak their hands places they probably shouldn't in public. Nick laughed, and we goofed on all of them.

That was the last time Nick and I really did anything together. He started hanging with sketchier and sketchier people, and Mom wouldn't let me go anywhere with him alone. Nick had always seemed like he was too large, too much for his own life. But then everything about Nick started to shrink. Now with Nick gone, I'm just a girl skating backward, only I don't have a partner.

Sincerely,

Brynn

Folder: Drafts
To: Rachel@msnbc.com
From: Brynnieh0401@gmail.com
Date: September 22
Subject: Mommy and Me

Dear Rachel Maddow,

Today is Mom and Fart Weasel's anniversary. They have actually only been bound on a federal and cosmic level for two years. But Fart took a shower, and Mom folded a nice dress into a duffel bag to change into after her shift, so shit's getting swanky up in here.

My dad used to make a big deal out of their anniversary. He would wear a tie, and Mom would put on makeup and twist her hair into a perfect, shiny bun. I would raise my arms like I wanted to be picked up, and when Mom hugged me, I would shove my nose into her hair. The soft, sweet oil that smoothed down her chocolate-brown wisps smelled like Easter candy. My chubby little fingers messed it up. She didn't yell, though. I think she liked me snuggling into her head. She'd laugh and push me off on Nick and pop into the bathroom to redo it.

That's how it was with Mom and me, up until Nick started to go downhill. Mom went down with him. My grandma, her mom, was really mean. Like, beat you and call you fat and leave all the money to her church and none to her only daughter kind of mean. She bounced back from that, a little, when she married my dad. She was pretty good at being a wife, and a mom to little Nicky and then to surprise but much-hoped-for baby Brynn. Mom went to night school to become a registered nurse and worked part-time when I started kindergarten. But Mom was tethered to us, to Nick in particular. Babies are supposed to be cut off from the mom and then both of them get to be separate people. That didn't happen with Mom and Nick. His blood was her blood, his grades were her grades, his wrestling injuries were bullets to her brain.

Maybe there are guys who could understand this. Dad wasn't one of them. He got angrier and angrier with Nick, which Mom took personally. She felt like when Dad was mad at Nick, Dad was mad at *her*. There was nothing pretty, nothing soft about the last few months before Dad peeled out of our driveway. With these pieces of her ripped away, she bled and bled until there was little of the mom I knew left. Maybe Mom found Fart Weasel because he had already settled at rock bottom; at least she knew where he stood from the beginning, so there were no new failures to slice her apart. Maybe she ignores me because I am the last thing that can really ruin her.

Sometimes I wish I could just bury my face in her hair and I'd look up and be ten again and the last few years would all be a horrible, sucky dream. But Mom won't let me close enough to even try.

Sincerely,

Brynn

Folder:	Drafts
To:	Rachel@msnbc.com
From:	Brynnieh0401@gmail.com
Date:	September 24
Subject:	Lost and found or just lost maybe

Dear Rachel Maddow,

I finally worked up the nerve to take the long route past Sarah's locker today. It's the particularly scenic way because her homeroom is on the second floor of the building and mine is two floors below.

In a different wing.

She was there. I stopped a few feet away, trying to look engrossed in a hygiene poster. But of course I stared at her. Her blond hair brushed her shoulders. She had a pencil stuck behind her ear. She was biting the eraser of another pencil looking up at the sky, lost in thought. I traced her body with my eyes. I missed her narrow shoulders and her narrow waist and at this moment even her narrow little way of seeing the world. What would it take to go over there and just ask her what she thought of the growing size of the Republican districts in Pennsylvania?

She looked up at me suddenly, as if psychically called by the thought of another GOP win come midterms. Our eyes locked. But she frowned and shook her head a little. We both knew I was far afield of where I belonged. Or at least she did. She turned away and went into a classroom, and I slunk down to mine. Where we both knew I mattered more than up there.

Or at least I did.

Sincerely,

Brynn

Folder:	Drafts
To:	Rachel@msnbc.com
From:	Brynnieh0401@gmail.com
Date:	September 25
Subject:	Friends

Dear Rachel Maddow,

Is it hard to be famous? Like, does that net you more or fewer friends? You aren't an actress or whatever. You're *you* on TV. Well, you're *you* with makeup and no glasses and perfect hair, but still. It's not like people think they are meeting a character when they see you on the street who are then shocked and come away thinking, "Actually, she's kind of a dumb-ass who isn't that into politics."

At least, I don't think they do. Maybe they are just like, "Huh, I thought she'd be wearing a blazer."

Does fame bring you a better quality of friends? Nick's friends all kind of sucked. Tip from me to you: Being well known for scoring a high does not gain you a lot of quality associations. Most of the assholes didn't even come to his funeral. Granted, Nick's parole officer was there and a lot of them probably had stuff to hide, but still. Only two of them, Leigh and Erin, bothered to speak to me.

"Hey, kid," I think Leigh had said first.

"Hi, honey," said Erin.

I could count on one hand the number of times we'd spoken before this. "Hi?" I tried.

"Listen, this sucks donkey dicks," said Leigh.

Erin elbowed him in his side. "What Leigh means is that we're sorry. Nick really was a great guy. Even lately . . ."

This was one hot mess of a nice gesture. He hadn't been great for a long time. We all knew that. And yet, here were two people who had also lost Nick trying to be nice to me, so I wanted them to keep talking forever.

"No, really, Brynn. Really. We saw him, what? A month or two ago? And he talked about you. He was proud you were still in school and on the honor roll. He was real proud of that." Erin had shaken her head.

"Okay" was all I could think of.

"Here, kid. Take this." Leigh shoved a folded piece of paper into my hand. "These are our numbers. Text us yours and we'll keep an eye on you. It's only right."

"Okay," I said again.

They nodded and went to pay their respects to Nick's closed casket.

Not long after that Mom had fainted. Honest to God I think she was faking. But Fart Weasel made a big show over her and growled at me that I had to come home with them. How messed up is that? Though at least they both came to the funeral.

Unlike Dad.

Sitting here, two years later, dictating this to my laptop, really brings it home. Nick is not coming back. That's why it's nice to know you, Rachel. You'll be there to talk to me for an hour, give or take commercials. Being famous makes you a friend to people you don't even know about! A friend to shitty, lame-ass people like me, maybe, but that's what a lot of regular people have anyway. So. Thanks for that.

Sincerely,

Brynn

Folder: Drafts
To: Rachel@msnbc.com
From: Brynnieh0401@gmail.com
Date: September 26
Subject: Dead air

Dear Rachel Maddow,

Mr. Grimm is still on my case about writing back to you. He said it would be polite to send you a brief follow-up e-mail. I will answer you, but it might take me a while. My brother died two years ago today. September 26 always sneaks up on me and jumps me in the bathroom. I need to hide out someplace for a while.

Sincerely,

Brynn

Folder:	Inbox
To:	Brynnieh0401@gmail.com
From:	**Mail Delivery Subsystem** <mailer-daemon@googlemail.com>
Date:	September 27
Subject:	Hi Dad

Delivery to the following recipient failed permanently
RaymondHarper4509@gmail.com
Technical details of permanent failure:
Google tried to deliver your message, but it was
rejected by the server for the recipient domain
gmail.com
by gmail-smtp-in.1.google.com. [2a00:1490:400c:c0b::1b].
The error that the other server returned was:
550-5.1.1 The e-mail account that you tried to reach
does not exist. Please try
550-5.1.1 double-checking the recipient's e-mail
address for typos or
550-5.1.1 unnecessary spaces. Learn more at
550 5.1.1 https://support.google.com/mail/answer/6596
c67si9004821wma.125-gsmtp

——Original message——

Dear Dad,

It's been a few years. I don't know if this is still your e-mail address. I found it on a card in the desk. I'm a junior in high school now. You've missed a few birthdays. And Christmases. And Easters. And school plays, awards banquets, softball games, and debate competitions. Oh, and Nick's funeral. Don't worry—I don't really celebrate any of those things anymore, so you don't have to feel guilty about not contacting me.

And Nick's already dead, so he isn't going to have another funeral.

I hope you are happy with your new family. Your wife is damn pretty.

And your little girl and baby boy, too. I liked looking at their pictures until you blocked me or deleted your account online or whatever.

Did you know I was looking at the public photos?

Were you afraid I'd show up one day and want to play happy family?

Don't worry. I'll stay in the one you helped destroy.

Fuck you, Dad.

Sincerely,

Brynn

Folder:	Drafts
To:	Rachel@msnbc.com
From:	Brynnieh0401@gmail.com
Date:	September 29
Subject:	Family Ties

Dear Rachel Maddow,

Stepparents get a bad rap. Stepmothers, actually. But let me tell you, in my experience, *stepfathers* deserve all the shade thrown at them from every direction. Or at least mine does.

I mean, I never liked the guy. I never even tried—this is true. But he never tried, either. And he never cared about me or Nick and who knows about Mom. And he's the grown-ass adult and I am a kid, and grown-ass adults are supposed to be better.

Today's interaction with the Failed (Grown) Ass (Adult):

Me: Do we have any bread?

Him: Did you buy any?

Me: No.

Him: Do you have money to buy any?

Me: How could I?

Him: Quit fucking loafing and maybe then you'd have some goddamn bread.

Me: *snort*

Him: You think that's funny? Get a job.

Rachel, he failed to realize his lame pun. This kind of stupid pissed me off as much as not being able to make even a fucking PB&J. PB&J should be a human right. Or whatever the cultural equivalent of a PB&J is all over the world.

At least I could hide in my room with the peanut butter and eat it straight out of the jar with a spoon. It could be worse.

Sincerely,

Brynn

Folder:	Inbox
To:	Brynnieh0401@gmail.com
From:	**Mail Delivery Subsystem** <mailer-daemon@googlemail.com>
Date:	October 3
Subject:	Making contact

Delivery to the following recipient failed permanently
RayNHarp0945@gmail.com
Technical des of permanent failure:
Google tried to deliver your message, but it was
rejected by the server for the recipient domain gmail.
com
by gmail-smtp-in.l.google.com. [2a00:0973:400c:c0b::1b].
The error that the other server returned was:
550-5.1.1 The e-mail account that you tried to reach
does not exist. Please try
550-5.1.1 double-checking the recipient's e-mail
address for typos or
550-5.1.1 unnecessary spaces. Learn more at
550 5.1.1 https://support.google.com/mail/answer/6596
c43si9004801wma.125-gsmtp

——Original message——

Hi Dad,
I got this e-mail from an old permission slip. I have tried to contact you at
another old e-mail, but I guess you don't have that address anymore? How
does an e-mail address go away? Physical mail you can forward, I know.
And phone numbers are reassigned. But, do you close an e-mail account?
To avoid that? Or maybe you block certain people?

Anyway, I thought you might want to know how I'm doing. That I'm
still alive and kicking. And maybe you'd like to see me again? I'm not so

bad, am I? Unlike Nick, I neither drink nor do drugs. I don't have the stomach for either. And I write a lot of letters.

Do you remember that about me? That I liked to write? Do you remember the newspapers I'd made for you and Mom and Nicholas? I could teach your kids to do that. I could be a good influence. If you'd let me.

Sincerely,

Brynn

Folder: Inbox
To: Brynnieh0401@gmail.com
From: Egrimm@westing.pa.edu
Date: October 5
Subject: RE: Questions

Dear Rachel Maddow,

~~I took a few days off from la escuela because Nick is still dead and Sarah hates me and what's the point? But unfortunately Mom forced me to go back. She doesn't want me around on her day off so she can be loud with Fart Weasel. She actually said that to me. I don't know if she intended to disgust me out of bed, but that's what she succeeded in doing.~~ [Brynn— have you considered availing yourself of the guidance counselor? Please stop and see me after class.]

Within the first fifteen minutes of class, Mr. Grimm gently but repeatedly noted how thoughtful it was for you to have written back to me, and that the "courtesy of my reply" to you might be "therapeutic." When I told him I couldn't think of what to write (that was fit to send), Mr. Grimm gave me a list of questions to answer about myself for you. As if you don't have better things to do than read this.

1. Are you who you want to be?

I don't know who I want to be, but if I think about it—no. How could I want to be . . . what I am now? I can tell you who I used to be. That might be more interesting. In ninth grade I was still an Honors student. I was on the debate team. The newspaper and debate people were pretty much the same, and they liked to sit around talking about politics and world leaders and how the world was going to hell. I didn't like doing that. My mom and dad had gotten divorced, Nick died, and we had to move to a crappy house in ~~East Bumblefuck, Pennsyltucky~~. [What is another way you could describe our rural, economically depressed region?] I couldn't deal with the world's problems. I had too many of my own.

What kept me going for a while was the fact that I was also totally falling in love with the queen of the ninth-grade nerds, Sarah Livingston. I told Sarah I loved her on Halloween of freshman year. We were at a school dance. I pulled her over to the coatroom (the closet . . . I know, right?) and said it just like that. "I love you, Sarah." I do that. Tell people how I feel. It's like a nervous tick.

She looked kind of shocked at first, but then *she* pulled *me* behind a rack of parkas and we made out until her dad came to give us a ride home. She was my girlfriend ever since then. I think she came out to her parents right after that, and they seemed cool with it. I never told Mom, because then I'd have been killed or rehomed with weirdos from the Internet or something.

We were together from that day freshman year until this past summer, when she dumped me. I was "too much drama" for her. She had to focus on graduating in the top ten of our class and shoving her nose up whoever's ass was most useful at the time. I gave up on that kind of thing not long after I started dating Sarah. Even though I gradually slipped away from the Honors/AP crowd and even the Academic crowd, it was still enough for almost two years that I could make Sarah laugh, that I was the chill one while she was the one bent on Making the World a Better Place. But then it wasn't.

Who I am now? I don't even know. My ability to care started to erode the day Nick died and washed away completely after I was kicked off the paper. Since I hate being home, I mostly go hide in the library at school or the nice, big one downtown. I like listening to books about faraway worlds that exist only in the imagination. Or I watch or listen to you. You are a debate and newspaper kid all grown up, and you know what you are talking about. It freaks me out, all the shit going on in the world. But you are so cheerful when you talk about it. Like maybe there is something to be hopeful about. If I could be anything, maybe I would be that. Hopeful. Someone who could give hope to someone else.

My computer time is up and thank God, because if I ever sent this, I have driven well past the borders of overshare city a million times by now. ~~Hello, Rachel Maddow intern! I hope you likey the melodrama!~~ [Brynn, your candor is powerful, and I appreciate your attempt at answering these questions. But keep in mind your audience might benefit from more exposition and different language to appreciate your points? I'm just spitballing here. Please see me either before the school day begins or after class.]

Sincerely,

Brynn

Folder: Drafts
To: Rachel@msnbc.com
From: Brynnieh0401@gmail.com
Date: October 9
Subject: Breaking news

Dear Rachel Maddow,

I usually don't have news that is late breaking, so much as old news that breaks things. Like my heart, for instance.

Today Sarah wore a pink cardigan over a black tank top. It was warm, so she also wore a skirt. Girls in skirts kill me.

She was talking to Nancy, another friend I had when I was in newspaper. They were kind of whispering and giggling, and Nancy slipped her arm around Sarah's waist.

Girls who move on to other girls also kill me.

Sincerely,

Brynn

Folder:	Drafts
To:	Rachel@msnbc.com
From:	Brynnieh0401@gmail.com
Date:	October 10
Subject:	Questions

Dear Rachel Maddow,

Question two that Mr. Grimm suggested I answer for you: Do you like school? No. Not even a little.

Even if I thought about trying to learn something at school on purpose, the blue room curriculum isn't exactly enthralling. Lacey makes it *almost* bearable, but she is busy helping other people most of the time. And of course school sucks mostly because Sarah is there and she won't even look at me. Ace reporter Justin told me that Sarah left the paper to devote her time to Student Government. I knew that she was going to do that, as she never stopped talking about it over the summer. She thought conquering important issues like the environmental impact of cafeteria trays and serving locally sourced foods at the school dance would lead to Bigger Things.

Sadly, she was the only one I would ever talk to about Nick. She was the one who knew everything. I desperately wanted to text her to freak out about his two-year absence. How it had been so long and not long at all.

But I knew she wouldn't want my current "drama" popping her bubble of Important Life Work.

To make matters even better today at school, Nancy, the woman possibly vying for the position of Brynn 4.0 in Sarah's heart (less drama, more GPA points), stopped me in the hallway to sign a petition about the stupid trays.

"Don't bother with her," said Adam, current SGA vice president and unbearable human being. "She won't care."

"Issues affect us all, Adam," she said. I looked at her for a second, and then at him, to see if they'd acknowledge that I was a person they used to hang out with. That maybe I was a thinking, feeling human being even if I wasn't in Honors classes anymore.

They did not.

"I like trays. They can be used as weapons," I said, and kept walking.

"See? What'd I tell you?" said Adam.

I spun around to face him. Adam was thin, so thin. Part of me wondered if he wasn't such an ass because he was hungry all of the time. He was tall compared to the rest of his wrestler dude bros. His dark, wavy hair was piss-me-off perfect. "Does it bother you that presidential authority goes unchecked these days, and that we are basically fighting a third world war and barely even a peep, a *peep* I tell you, is heard from Congress? No? I doubt it. Because you are too busy worrying about trays."

Nancy's eyes went all wide, and Adam just rolled his. I had been listening to your audiobook, Rachel, to keep me company the last few nights. It all kind of came to me in that moment.

"Maybe you should tell your dealer to stop giving you the cheap stuff. 'Cause you're going mental."

I strode back to him and stood there, eye to eye now. Whether he was a wrestling god or not, I was angry and didn't care. I could take him. "Take it back," I said.

He had gotten to me and we both knew it, but he had fired the first shot before I could dodge.

"What?" He smirked. "Going to run home and cry to your big brother? Oh, wait. That won't work." He laughed then. It sounded choked, like he was trying to be a hard-ass but couldn't quite pull it off.

I stepped back, shocked. Westing was a small town where everyone knew everyone. That was a low blow. Nick had been a friend of Adam's older brother, so Adam knew him, too.

"Adam!" snapped Nancy. "What are you doing?" I felt her put her hand on my shoulder. "Brynn, just go. I'm sorry."

Nick told me once that Adam's dad terrorized Adam and his brothers. That I should steer clear of all of them because they couldn't help but be mean assholes bent on winning whatever prize was put in front of them. I knew something about Fathers Who Suck, but this was not winning any sympathy from me at the moment.

Just then, a teacher rounded the corner and looked at us.

"Is there a problem here?" he said.

I didn't bother to argue. I just shook my head and got the hell out of there.

Sincerely,

Brynn

Folder:	Drafts
To:	Rachel@msnbc.com
From:	Brynnieh0401@gmail.com
Date:	October 11
Subject:	No frills

Dear Rachel Maddow,

I had scheduled a lot of sulking for most of my peer mentor time today.

"Is it the work, Brynn? Because honestly Mr. Grimm would be happy if you wrote a paragraph or two for this essay," Lacey said. "I see you dictating to your laptop all the time. I see you *typing*. Why are you refusing to do this? Do you have something against"—she glanced at my binder—"the Free Exercise Clause?"

"Of course not," I said.

"Then why are there no sentences for me to edit? You could lead with that. 'I have nothing against the Free Exercise Clause.' Thesis statement. Boom."

I sighed. "Can I ask you a question?"

"Is it about the First Amendment?"

"No."

"I will answer one question of your choosing for every sentence you write," she said.

I typed, "The Free Exercise Clause is a good idea because you can worship Satan if you want to."

Lacey sighed. "Well, it's not inaccurate."

"Does it bug you if people think you are . . ." I searched for words. What did Adam think I was? Stupid? Worthless? "Not worth their respect?"

Lacey sat quietly for a minute. "Is this about Sarah?" she said.

"No. I mean . . . no. Something else."

"I guess I quit caring what other people thought a long time ago."

"Yeah. But what if they get in your face?"

Lacey pointed to my laptop.

"It's not that Satanism is the best religion; it's the idea that a person should not be stopped from observing their beliefs by the government," I read aloud as I typed.

"People generally don't get in my face. Sometimes they stare. Sometimes they pretend I'm not there. It can be annoying, but mostly I have my own thing going on." Lacey shrugged.

"Yeah," I said.

"Ignore the jerks, Brynn," said Lacey. "They aren't worth your time."

"Okay, peer mentor," I said.

"Now write your essay. I *will* care if you make me look bad. You *should* worry about that."

"All right, all right."

I wrote enough to make Lacey happy.

Who cared what stupid Adam thought?

I did. At least a little.

Because I knew Sarah thought like Adam a lot of the time.

I shouldn't care about her, either.

But I did.

At least a little.

Or a lot.

Sincerely,
Brynn

Folder:	Inbox
To:	Brynnieh0401@gmail.com
From:	Egrimm@westing.pa.edu
Date:	October 11
Subject:	RE: Questions

Dear Rachel Maddow,

Mr. Grimm asked me, "What are you passionate about?" Not to sound too pathetic again but, currently, nothing. Before, I'd say I was passionate about my family. [Good.] I had it pretty good for about a decade. I loved those stupid people. Mom was an amazing nurse, and Dad worked the Bar, Rod, and Wire division at the steel plant. Mom quit when Nick was first caught with Oxy, and that actually went okay. Dad still made good money. Nick went to some wilderness place that made him see that Selling Was Bad. But then Dad lost his job and thought Mom was being too easy on Nick. He tried his own version of "tough love," but Nick hated that and went back to making fast money. He could buy his Xbox games or whatever without Dad yelling at him to get a real job. So Nick kept getting kicked out of the house. Mom freaked, Dad left, Dad came back, Mom slept with the Fart Weasel . . . or something like that. My grandparents are all dead, and I'd never heard good things about them anyway. Now it's just a big heaping pile of shit, my family. [You know what, Brynn? I'm not going to delete text anymore. You have a lot of difficult things to express and expletives help you do that clearly. However, you do realize you are turning this in to a teacher and (in theory) a public news figure, yes?]

"Brynnie, as soon as you turn eighteen, you will come live with me," Nick said the last time I saw him. "You and me against the world." He smiled. Even with his weird pointy teeth, he still had a great smile.

"Sure," I said. "We'll have our own place with the best parties. I'll make buffalo chicken dip for the games, and we will witness the Steelers crush the Patriots' football dynasty once and for all."

"Damn right, kid," he said. He slung his black leather jacket over his shoulder and stuck a cigarette in his mouth. He was like a short, fat, stoned James Dean. He died a week later. I can't even think about buffalo anything now without wanting to puke.

I know, Rachel, you're a Patriots fan. But don't worry. No one's perfect. [Truth.]

Sincerely,
Brynn

Folder: Inbox
To: Brynnieh0401@gmail.com
From: Egrimm@westing.pa.edu
Date: October 12
Subject: RE: Questions

Dear Rachel Maddow,

"What bothers you?" Mr. Grimm asked me. I think this is meant to be an inspiring political question for your sake. [Yes.] But. [Sigh.] Everything around me bothers me. I live amidst trees. Not pretty trees, but ugly evergreens that would really benefit from shedding their needles and getting new ones in the spring. The people here in Westing bother me, too, because they are kinda like the trees. We'd all be better off if we burst into flames like a phoenix and got up stark naked out of the ashes with soft, fluffy feathers. Instead, the cold gets to you and then the heat gets to you, and pretty soon you forget the blue sky goes up forever, and your gaze doesn't lift above the billboard for the dairy that closed a decade ago. Even the crowd I used to run with is a lot like that. Sarah swore she'd get out of this town and go to an Ivy League and Save Us All. But will she? She probably will. Her dad worked steel like mine. Now he's a greeter at the Walmart. That will probably make good admissions essay fodder. [Honestly? You are probably right.]

Today I passed Sarah as she was asking people to sign yet another petition.

"Brynn," she said warmly. I'd say she sounded like a newscaster, but I wouldn't want to insult you.

"Oh, we're talking now, are we?" I said.

She flinched a little. Crimson crept from her ears to color her face the same shade as her skirt. She had her hair up in a perfect blond power ponytail. Strands of golden yellow framed her face. The sight of her engaging in civic involvement was so enticing I wanted her to grab me and kiss me and swear she'd never leave me again. [Evocative. Please, Brynn, let's spare the evocative in assignments turned in and save it for your obviously colorful memoir.]

"Brynn," she said again instead. "There is something incredibly important happening. The school board has decided to let a student join the committee to choose a new school superintendent. Do you know what that *means*?"

"I assume it means that the school board is going to let a student help choose the new school superintendent, Sarah," I said.

"Yes. So, obviously this individual should represent the entire student body. We have to make sure the right person is chosen."

I didn't care in the least, but I nodded anyway.

"So will you sign?" She thrust her clipboard at me.

A long paragraph at the top of the page was typed in, I swear, five-point font. I squinted at it. "What does this say?" I bent down, trying to read the words. "We the student body recognize the importance for a thoughtful, nuanced voice to represent us . . .' "

"Just sign it, Brynn. I told you what it said." She sighed. "Pretty please?" she said in her you'll-do-this-if-you-love-me voice. Now I was the one who flinched.

"Wait a minute," I said, still reading. "This basically says you want only an *Honors* student on this committee?"

"Well, yes, of course," she said.

God, she was also cute when she was about to get pissy.

She was cute a lot around me these days.

"But I know all of you, and let me tell you, you don't represent anybody but yourselves," I said. It was true. The last time Sarah and the Honors kids were in charge of anything, homecoming and school spirit week planning devolved into a lot of shouting about funding for the public good. It annoyed the hell out of me even though I was the biggest fan Sarah and public services ever had. And I *hate* pep rallies with the fiery heat of a thousand toasters. Rachel, you and I know that if someone is elected to serve a constituency, she should represent the will of the people who elected her. And the Westing High people love themselves the shit out of football and cheerleaders. SGA thus had an obligation to provide pointless dress-up days and wig contests, but they failed to do so.

Not cool, school elected representatives. Not cool.

And word on the street (and by "street" I mean "a really freckled kid named Justin") had it that the Honors cohort was gunning for a new Honors lounge and funding for exclusive field trips, among other perks not available to the masses.

"But, Brynn"—back was Sarah's if-you-loved-me voice—"we are Honors students for a reason."

"Luck," I said.

"No, dear," she said. "Or everybody would be here."

Yeah, because that's how luck works.

I rolled my eyes and gave her back the clipboard. "Have Nancy sign it. I'm sure she supports your cause."

Sarah frowned but said nothing.

This bothers me, Rachel. All of it. And it bothers me more that I have no idea how to change it. [This is great! Not only did you answer one of the questions, you have also pulled in your critical thinking skills on civic engagement! Also, it's probably best if you speak with some of those resource people to whom I referred you about your romantic relationships and keep them out of your work.]

Sincerely,

Brynn

Folder:	Drafts
To:	Rachel@msnbc.com
From:	Brynnieh0401@gmail.com
Date:	October 15
Subject:	Home on the range

Dear Rachel Maddow,

Last year on this date, at this time, I would have been at Sarah's house. But since there is no more Sarah, I am stuck at home. On the plus side, Fart Weasel was out buying a new hose (probably to use in strangling someone's dreams). On the minus side, Mom stayed behind.

"Get up, Brynn. It's past ten," she said from the doorway.

I just mumbled into my pillow. There was no reason I should get up. I had no one to call, nowhere to go, nothing I wanted to do.

"Brynn. Get your lazy ass out of bed." She came over and batted at my blanketed feet.

I squirmed away from her, but I only have a twin bed, so there wasn't much room for escape. "Mph, sleep. I wanna sleep forever."

"I haven't slept in since you were born. Get. Up." She didn't leave until I sat up. I got dressed and trudged into the kitchen. Mom eyed me.

"So, any big plans for today?" I asked. I thought maybe a friendly approach would make her ignore me quicker.

"Brynn . . ." she started. She sighed. Then she sighed again. Then she triple sighed and I knew I was in for it. "What are you doing? You should have a job. You should have plans for your future. You should have any kind of ambition at all. Nicky didn't . . ."

It was as if he entered the room, then. The temperature dropped twenty degrees, his icy corpse floating just outside our peripheral vision. The fact was that I never cared about what Mom or Dad and certainly not Fart Weasel thought of me. But I wanted to make Nick proud. He always saw the best in me, so I wanted to be the best. I thought if I tried hard for the both of us, then maybe he'd want to make *me* proud of *him* again.

Before I could do enough, he gave up. Or couldn't fight the drugs, or whatever. I still wondered that if I'd been a better sister, maybe he'd still be here.

Maybe Mom wondered that. Maybe she felt responsible for Nick's death, just like me.

"Do you ever feel like Nick would still be alive if you were a better mom?" I asked. Maybe we could have a Hallmark moment of shared grief or some shit that would bring us together as mother and daughter.

Mom's eyes grew huge and round. She raised her hand to her chest and stepped away from me, like my words punched her. "I did everything. Everything for him. For you. How . . ."

Definitely no Hallmark moment here.

"No, I didn't mean it like *that*," I said. "I just mean, I don't know, that *I* think I could have . . ."

"Stop. Just stop."

"Listen! I'm not saying I think Nick died because you screwed up! I'm saying—"

"Brynn!" Mom shouted. She wouldn't let me explain.

"Mom!" I shouted back, but Fart Weasel banged in the back door. Mom conveniently burst into tears as soon as she saw him.

"What'd you do now?" he said, looking at me.

"Just go," Mom said, through muffled sobs.

I grabbed my jacket and backpack off the shelf in the hall and ran off the porch before they changed their minds and made me stay.

I don't know if it was my fault Nick died. Or Mom's, or Dad's. It probably was at least a little Fart Weasel's. But the giant hole he left was big enough for me to slip through. I could hide behind and in his memory. Mom couldn't see me there, nor could I see myself. There was only the empty Nick-shaped void where he should have been.

Sincerely,
Brynn

Folder:	Drafts
To:	Rachel@msnbc.com
From:	Brynnieh0401@gmail.com
Date:	October 16
Subject:	Good times

Dear Rachel Maddow,

October used to be my favorite month. The wind whips bloodred and sunset-orange and lemon-yellow leaves through the air and hides all the gray. It's some picturesque-ass shit if you ask me.

Sarah was my October year-round. She is picturesque as fuck, true. And God knows she can stir chills in me. But it was more that she was a crisp sense of possibility. She was a fresh-lined sheet of loose-leaf and a perfectly sharpened pencil.

Back in the early days, we had a routine. I'd go over to her house. We'd read each other passages from *It Takes a Village* and vow that we'd be the women leaders of the next generation. She'd try to talk me into doing my homework, and I'd try to talk her out of doing hers. She'd let me talk about Nick. She seemed to understand that reading and writing and math took me five times as long as it did anyone else in my class. That letters turned in funny ways and numbers looked like a foreign alphabet. She got that all of my energy for school died with Nick. So we'd end up in a tickle fight, and then we'd start kissing and then. Well. Let's just say the sky was blue over every perfect autumn day right there in her room.

Sarah was . . . is . . . generous. If she considers you to be hers, then she hates your enemies and loves your friends. She loathed Dad and Fart Weasel. She remembered Nick's birthday and even went to the cemetery twice when I went to stomp on the flowers I'd put on his grave.

But when one is *not* Sarah's, one simply is not. One ceases to exist. It meant so much to me to *matter* to her. She knew that. And to then not matter? God. How can you do that to a person? I wasn't exactly the best girlfriend, but I loved her. And she left.

Typical of people, isn't it? Typical of life.

Fuck people. Fuck life.

This makes me know that we can't go back. I started not mattering even when we were together. That was worse than being alone,

I think.

Sincerely,

Brynn

Folder: Drafts
To: Rachel@msnbc.com
From: Brynnieh0401@gmail.com
Date: October 16
Subject: I might believe

Dear Rachel Maddow,

Are you religious? I'm not. Mom and Fart Weasel are, so that's enough to make me run from any church. Sarah used to say (maybe she still does, actually) that she's "spiritual." I don't know what that means. I don't think she really does, either. I think she just wanted to be able to hang with the kids who talked about Zen and finding yourself on a work trip over the summer or something.

I bring this up because something happened that made me think that maybe, just maybe, God is a thing. A real thing or idea or bearded guy in space just outside the Earth's atmosphere that today looked down and thought, "Brynn, you ridiculous little shit, maybe you should get a life." I know that people are starving or suffering, and the woes of a failing seventeen-year-old junior really aren't high on the priority list. But maybe God sneezed and accidently gave me the side-eye, and since he's God or whatever, he thought he'd throw something good my way for funsies.

Space God gave unto Brynn in study hall today. Lacey had just finished rattling off a fifteen-minute explanation of an algebra problem to us. It took her four tries until she found a way to explain it that we all understood.

"Honestly, why do you bother?" I asked her afterward. "When are we ever going to use this stuff in real life?"

"It's fun to explain things. You can practically see a light bulb flicker over Riley's head once he gets something."

"Isn't it boring as balls talking about the same thing over and over and over again?"

Lacey chuckled. "Nothing is ever boring with you, Brynn."

I opened my mouth to argue with her again, but stopped short when the door opened and in walked the most beautiful creature Space God had ever created.

"Um, hi?" the beautiful creature said. "Is this room zero-zero-five?"

I wondered at the notion that the blue room did, in fact, have a number.

"Yes." Ms. Yee, Applied math, science, and study hall enthusiast, smiled and got up from her chair. "Are you Michaela Jordan? Welcome!"

Michaela nodded. I watched her walk up to Ms. Yee and shake her hand. She was perfect. She had these light gray eyes that *pierced*. Damn.

"That's me," she said. She looked around the room. She smiled at Lacey and then glanced around, her gaze stopping on me. She smiled wider. I couldn't help but stare.

"Class, Michaela has joined us at Westing High after moving from . . ." Ms. Yee paused. "Michigan?"

Michaela nodded.

"She has been assigned to the blue room as a peer tutor. She's joining us for her free period, which happens to also be study hall for all of you. Let's be friendly. Michaela, feel free to have a seat wherever you want!" And Ms. Yee went back to her desk.

And Lacey went back to knowing everything.

And Michaela went to the back of the room to sit right in front of me.

I did not go back. For the first time in years, my brain moved on to new thoughts. Thoughts that made sitting in the uncomfortably confining blue room desks nearly impossible.

Oh my Space God. What the Space hell do I do now?

I have a best new thing in the world today, Rachel. This segment hasn't been on *The Brynn Harper* show in a long, long time.

Sincerely,

Brynn

Folder: Drafts
To: Rachel@msnbc.com
From: Brynnieh0401@gmail.com
Date: October 17
Subject: Belief, continued

Dear Rachel Maddow,

Michaela came back today. Michaela will come back every day. Michaela gave up her study hall to come peer tutor us, having been at Westing High only a week. She was a peer tutor at her school in Michigan. Michaela likes peer tutoring.

Michaela, Michaela, Michaela.

Today she helped Lance for twenty minutes on the intro paragraph to a persuasive essay.

Then she was going to help me with something, but instead Lacey checked Michaela's bio lab for her. It took Michaela like two minutes to figure out the awesome that is our blue room leader.

So she really is smart.

With curly dark hair and eyes that I swear fucking *twinkle*.

Michaela looked over to witness me totally creeping on her, and like always, she smiled. I tried to smile back, but I think my face didn't understand the messages coming from my brain, it was so out of practice. I just sort of grimaced.

Every day, she'll come back, Rachel. Every. Day.

Sincerely,

Brynn

Folder: Drafts
To: Rachel@msnbc.com
From: Brynnieh0401@gmail.com
Date: October 18
Subject: Every day

Dear Rachel Maddow,

Today, Michaela sat down next to *me*.

"Hi," she said.

"Um. Hi?" I said.

"Lacey said I should talk to you."

"Oh yeah. She gets sick of helping me with math all the time." I looked down at my hands.

"She didn't mention math."

I snuck a glance over at Lacey. She was noticeably turned toward the opposite side of the room.

"Oh."

"But I can help you with that if you want. I love math!" Michaela beamed.

"Okay." I prayed that Lacey hadn't exaggerated my conversational skills.

I didn't say much as Michaela bent over my math book, explaining a theorem to me. I watched as the black coils of her hair bounced when she moved her head.

"Are you listening to me?" she asked.

"No. I was too taken with your glorious hair. Also, your eyes," I said, nervous truth-spewing in full effect.

I could feel the heat in my face as I watched attractive red blotches rise on her neck.

"Oh, wow. Um. Thanks." She pulled at a dark lock next to her chin.

"But I'm impressed by your mathematical, uh, prowess. As well. You are impressive."

"Oh, wow. Um. Thanks," she said again.

If I kept speaking, I thought both of our heads might just spontaneously combust. Just then, the bell rang.

"Well. Okay. I'll see you guys tomorrow," she said, mostly to me. Lacey turned around and grinned. I just shook my head back at her, kind of stunned.

I don't know what the hell happened there, Rachel. Something. Something happened. But that's all the news that's fit to print at the moment.

Sincerely,
Brynn

Folder: Drafts
To: Rachel@msnbc.com
From: Brynnieh0401@gmail.com
Date: October 19
Subject: Freckle Juice

Dear Rachel Maddow,

If you are in the market for a relentless and indefatigable high school Intern, I know a guy.

"Brynn."

"Justin." We basically had a ritual greeting at this point.

"The paper—"

"Needs me. Only, yeah, no, it doesn't. I read your piece about cafeteria trays. Who knew it actually was better for the Earth." I rolled my eyes. "In the pocket of SGA now, are we?"

Justin grimaced. "Listen. I stand by the reporting on that. But I'm telling you, things are weird. Like, War Memorial weird. I've been working that story since it broke, and I think if you just look at all the accounts, you'd be able to see how conflicting everyone's explanations are. Maybe if you could just come down to the journalism room once in a while to visit?"

"No."

"Sarah's not even there anymore. You know that. Neither is Adam. Or Nancy."

I raised my eyebrows.

He shrugged. "This is not news to you. But what *could* be news is this War Memorial stuff. I think maybe even people we know could have been involved. People from here at school, Brynn."

A tiny spark of interest thrilled with in me. It quickly fizzled when I realized a 2.3 was still far away. I sighed. "I'll think about it."

"No, you won't. You are saying that to get rid of me."

"Well, okay. I probably won't. But Mr. McCloud would be there and

I can't look him in the face. I'm not trying to get rid of you. You could come down to the blue room sometime, you know."

Justin flushed red. "Oh. You think?"

"Yeah, sure. Why not? Nothing's stopping you."

Justin blushed again. "Maybe I will. Um. Lacey Willis is usually down there."

"Why, yes, she is, Justin." I looked at him again. "Oh my God. You're in love with Lacey."

"I'm not in love," he said defensively. "But you know she took Academic Bowl last year as captain. She'll probably do it again. That's hot. And then there are those dresses she always wears. . . ." He trailed off.

"Well, come on down, friend. I'll be your wingman." I grinned. All of that *was* hot, I had to agree. Justin was a dude and actually had a shot with woefully straight Lacey, damn him.

Watch this space, Rachel.

Sincerely,

Brynn

Folder: Drafts
To: Rachel@msnbc.com
From: Brynnieh0401@gmail.com
Date: October 20
Subject: Downtown

Dear Rachel Maddow,

Since Mom and Fart Weasel were both home in the hours before I had to go to work, I decided to walk around near the War Memorial.

The whole place smelled like summer camp—damp and woody, with whiffs of smoke still hanging around the massive tarps half-heartedly covering gaping holes. Strange dark swirls formed a maze in parts of the stubby yard next to the river and spread out into the parking lot.

It'd have been kind of cool in a movie. In real life, it just sucked.

What the fuck had happened here? I remembered Justin had said he'd thought the whole silence around it was odd.

But I couldn't go down that hole with him until I was sure I wasn't going to flunk out for good.

Although, aside from who had set the fire or why, how did it burn so quickly? Maybe they used cheap stuff when they redid the front of the building and that helped destroy the place. I should tell Justin to look into that angle. *That* would be a story, if the contractor ripped off the city and then . . .

No. Just cut it out, Brynnie. Leave this to the paper people or the police or the city managers. You have underwear to sell.

Though maybe I'd just text Justin my thought.

He was probably bored over the weekend and could use the distraction.

I was doing this for *him*. Because of my generous nature.

Sincerely,

Brynn

Folder: Drafts
To: Rachel@msnbc.com
From: Brynnieh0401@gmail.com
Date: October 21
Subject: 34C

Dear Rachel Maddow,

It's been three days since my last unfortunate attempt at speaking to Michaela. I think I might have freaked her out, because she didn't try it again. I do seem to catch her looking at me a fair amount, which technically might be construed as *her* catching *me* doing the looking.

Potayto, potahto, amiright, Rachel?

Since speaking didn't go so great, it is probably just as well I only watch her talk to everyone else and help them diagram sentences and solve problems and be wonderful. She watches me watching her like a mirror reflecting a mirror into awkward infinity. It might be nice to have her help me with my work, but that would require words to exit my mouth and reach her ears.

Her glorious, perfect ears.

I was content to let this continue, but several major developments occurred over the last week that have conspired to make life both more awesome and more absurd. First, Mom said I would no longer be getting food until I cleaned out my closet. While digging through piles years' deep, I found the pair of pants I had worn to Nick's funeral. They were almost comically small, but I couldn't bring myself to stuff them into the donation bag. I looked through the pockets and found Erin's and Leigh's phone numbers crumpled in the back. I called Erin on a whim, after all this time.

As it turned out, it was still her phone number. And she remembered me.

I met Erin for pizza that evening and she paid, and she said I could come over to the place she shares with Leigh anytime.

Erin then convinced me that I should take a job at Aerie with her. Aerie, if you don't know, Rachel, is the underwear branch of American Eagle.

A person might argue that this is the absolute last place I would ever want to work.

Particularly if this person was me.

But. Money is money. And it's not like I had anything to do other than sit in my room at home and miss Nick or Sarah or perhaps my life.

I know little about what undergarments people want to purchase, but I have quickly learned that all you really need to know to work at Aerie is how to fold thongs and how not to beat the crap out of tweeny girls.

I've worked two evenings already and intend to save most of my money so that I can move out of la casa de Fart Weasel as soon as humanly possible.

Today I was at Aerie with Erin, wondering again at the serendipitous misfortune that led me to be amidst the bralettes. Erin is actually a pretty good manager, so I try to work hard when she is on.

"Stack the undies those girls messed up, Brynn," she said as she walked by me. I was already beginning to hate the drawers full of under-stocked items. They are constantly a mess. Why people don't just take the hanging ones I don't understand. I stooped low over some push-up scoops when someone politely coughed behind me. I straightened and rammed my head into the bra rack on the way up.

"Son of a . . ." I rubbed my forehead, grateful I didn't take out an eye. "Damn it," I cursed the several halters knocked to the ground by the force of my head.

"You work here?" said a voice. I remembered the coughing person who had caused my near decapitation in the first place. Whom should I behold standing there, Rachel? Michaela, holding Blakely Lace Trim Lightly Lined in two shades. She was rubbing the edge of the Silver Shadow. Dear All the Stars in the Milky Way.

"Um. Yes. Lingerie enthusiast here," I said. Oh, Rachel, what the hell? I flushed *deep plum*. Michaela raised one eyebrow at me.

"Ah. Could you tell me where the dressing room is?"

"Sure," I said. My legs, still functional somehow, wobbled toward the back of the store. She followed me. I reached the row of blond-wood doors and pointed. She went into one. I watched her. My legs, having given their all, moved no more.

"Are you going to come in?" she said.

Yes. Yes, I am, Michaela. Let me help you with those pesky clasps.

"Oh. No. Sorry. I . . . I'm sorry." I blushed again and backed away. I willed my legs to move me far from there. Fortunately I had to argue with a customer about returning underwear purchased last winter, so I didn't see her again. Although when I went to put away items left in the changing room, I noticed she had left behind *deep plum*. And that she was a 34C.

I felt guilty somehow for knowing that.

Sincerely,
Brynn

Folder: Drafts
To: Rachel@msnbc.com
From: Brynnieh0401@gmail.com
Date: October 23
Subject: Workin' it

Dear Rachel Maddow,

I got an A on my tectonic plates paper today, since Greg and Bianca taught me how to insert charts into a document. I thought charts were cheating, but Ms. Yee was so happy I used any data at all that she complimented my work three times. Note: You might want to tell anyone you know to move away from California. Data suggests that one day an earthquake is going to make it its own island nation state.

Actually, maybe that's what Californians want.

I happily assembled a sale display and thought about filling three-to-five pages with charts about shrinking rain forests for my next report. Maybe Michaela could proofread the non-chart portion of it for me, since sometimes my speech-to-text program goes rogue and does what it wants. Just then, I caught a glimpse of another natural disaster. Sarah walked past with another girl. My breath caught in my throat, but Sarah didn't notice me. I thanked my lucky charts and got to the back of the store to lie low as long as possible to avoid detection.

Soon it became obvious that the store was dead slow, so Erin let me leave early. I made it a point to practically run to the nearest exit to avoid anyone I knew. Of course that meant that Sarah was standing just outside the sliding glass doors.

"Oh," I said, nearly running into her. "Sorry."

"Oh, hey," she said brightly. "Did you see that someone put soap in the mall fountain?" She laughed. "You totally said you'd do that one day. I'm disappointed someone beat you to it!"

This was true. Nick and his friends had done it once. It was a pretty powerful mall fountain. The water shot up about ten feet in the air. The suds produced were pretty epic. I wanted to innovate and add food coloring, or maybe try some sort of scented pink bubble bath. But why did Sarah remember that? Why was she even talking to me?

I could practically see the same questions pop into Sarah's mind as I thought them. It was as if she had forgotten that we were no longer fun Sarah and Brynn for a moment.

"Guess I'll have to think of something else," I said.

"Yeah." She suddenly looked very uncomfortable.

"Aerie has bikinis on sale. Buy one piece, get the other free. They have your favorite shade of blue. There's one that's shimmery, like stars."

"Oh. Okay. Um. Thanks," she said.

I turned and walked toward the bus stop. I couldn't use my employee discount on sale items, so I didn't tell her I worked there.

Not that I'd buy her a bikini.

Not that I had even remembered that her favorite color was a navy "deep and dark like the night sky" at her favorite summer camp. Not that I remembered that fact because she said it to me as we lay on her Steelers blanket in her backyard, looking up at the stars. Not that I remembered that was the first time in forever that anyone told me they loved me and I knew it was true.

I mean, I barely remember anything about her.

Sincerely,

Brynn

Folder:	Drafts
To:	Rachel@msnbc.com
From:	Brynnieh0401@gmail.com
Date:	October 25
Subject:	Pay day

Dear Rachel Maddow,

I have stacks of sweet, sweet cash dollars. Well, maybe not stacks. Maybe I have like four twenty-dollar bills.

Still.

Since I'm not used to such riches, I splurged and bought a bouquet of yellow and white roses to put on Nick's grave. White and gold were Westing's colors, so I was technically trolling a dead guy, but he left me alone so fuck him. Enjoy your school spirit flowers, Nicky.

Maybe I should send some anonymously to Sarah.

I could walk to the cemetery after school and still get home by dark. It was kind of a hike, especially for me, but I hadn't gone to see him in a long time. The neatly lined rows of cool gray stone fanned out against glassy flat grass. I walked up the path, turned left, turned left again, past three tall trees whose leaves were also yellow.

I hoped the tree was trolling Nick, too.

Nick's tombstone stood plain next to my grandma's and grandpa's more ornate angel statues. It only had his name and dates; it had cost too much to chisel anything else onto it.

"Hey, Nicky," I said. I set the flowers down and traced my fingers along his name. Along the years of his birth and death and the dash in between.

Dash. That's all we do in this life. Dash here, dash there, dash our arms with needles, dash our days onto rock after we are gone.

"Miss you," I said to his grave. I never even met Mom's mom or dad, but I waved to their angels. They were family, after all.

"You're such a dick, you know that?" I shook my head and looked down at the ground. "I'm sorry. I'm so, so sorry." I stomped on him. "Asshole."

My eyes got a little blurry, so I decided to get out of there. "Sorry for the swears, Grandma and Grandpa," I said. A yellow leaf fluttered onto my hair.

That's all Nick could give me now. And all I could give him were flowers.

"I'll bring lilies next time," I said. Nick had always liked those at Easter.

Cemeteries are so orderly. Do they have to be that way? To fit everyone? Or are they like that because life is such a shitshow that at some point an ancient culture figured, "Hey, let's make death a little more tidy?"

I made a mental note to look that up at the library, even if I knew I didn't want to spend any more time thinking about cemeteries than I already did.

Sincerely,
Brynn

Folder: Drafts
To: Rachel@msnbc.com
From: Brynnieh0401@gmail.com
Date: October 26
Subject: Stairmaster

Dear Rachel Maddow,

Today Mr. Grimm sent me to the guidance counselor to drop off some forms. It's nice because I can take the back stairs to that office, and there is less risk of running into Sarah or Adam or most any other member of humanity.

However, the downside is that if someone wants to get quickly from their third-period class to the Applied mother ship, they would likely take the back stairwell. I was thus unprepared to note a halo of black curls descending in front of me as I retreated from the main hallway. They turned.

"Hi," Michaela said brightly.

"Oh," I said. Oh God. Why does she just suddenly appear in places that make perfect sense for her to be.

"How are you doing?"

Just say you're fine, Brynn. Just say it. It's what people do. Be a person, Brynn.

"Same old suck. Different day." I cringed a little at my words.

"Why?" she asked. She stopped on the last step.

"Um. Life?" I said. I could give exquisite detail. But I like to save sharing that sort of thing for cable news personalities.

Michaela considered me for a second. "Yeah," she said. "Fair enough."

I followed her into the hall.

"What do you do about life sucking?" she said.

"Complain to Lacey. Or to my computer. My computer is a great listener."

"I'll have to try that." Michaela laughed. "Have you ever considered talking to someone in addition to Lacey?"

"Like a shrink?" I rolled my eyes. "Yes. My mom took me to one after . . . uh . . . well, a while ago. And the lady was pretty judgy. I went to a nicer one, but then she moved to Texas. I just didn't go back."

"I actually meant talking to a friend. You could have two friends. Lacey and someone else."

We stopped in front of the blue room door.

"Oh. You mean someone who talks to me for free?"

"Something like that."

"Most people find me off-putting." That was one of Mom's kinder words for me.

"I don't," she said. "You could talk to me." She opened the blue room door. She stepped inside and turned a little toward me. She gave me a small smile.

I walked straight into the door Michaela held open for me.

I took my seat next to Lacey, ignoring the throbbing in my nose in an attempt to pretend I didn't constantly injure myself when Michaela came within three feet of me.

"Smooth," Lacey said.

"Shut up," I whispered.

I snuck a glance toward the back of the room. Michaela noticed and I swear to God she winked at me.

I decided not to leave my desk for the rest of the day. I'd probably fall in the Stoneycreek and take out some white-water rafters with me if she did that again.

Sincerely,

Brynn

Folder: Drafts
To: Rachel@msnbc.com
From: Brynnieh0401@gmail.com
Date: October 29
Subject: Workin' it

Dear Rachel Maddow,

Erin has talked me into working full weekends, so I'm making pretty good money at Aerie. (Well, okay, it's shitty money. But it's more than I've ever had to call my own before.) She likes me because I don't steal stuff and I don't sell pot like she suspects of the other three associates she just hired.

At school today Lacey and I got into kind of a fight, but it wasn't the Fart Weasel kind. It was the friend kind.

"Lacey, can't you just give me the stupid answer? I know you know it," I said.

"You have to show the work. Besides, you are supposed to learn this, I am not going to do it for you," her mechanical voice said for her. She has this actually programmed into her board, she says it in this room so much.

"Oh my God," I said.

"Just try. Try," she said.

"I will never use this in real life!"

"No, because we are all going to die here waiting for you to finish your stupid work!" This, also, should probably be a macro programmed into her board. "Brynn"—pause—"you are"—pause—"smart"—pause—"enough to do this"—pause—"on your own." She nudged the switch on her chair control and edged her wheel into my leg. I glared at her. She gave her most irritating grin.

"You are such a smart-ass," I said. She just rolled her eyes and then away from me.

"Language, Brynn," said Ms. Yee. I glared at her, too, but I stared at my paper for a while and solved for x eventually. Stupid x. Exes were hell in a number of areas in my life. I glared at Lacey for being right about me being able to do it on my own. The bell rang. On Fridays our teachers have a lunch meeting in the blue room, and we are forced into an "immersion" lunch. Why we can't eat in the yellow room or something I don't know. We met Lacey at the elevator and entered the cafeteria together. There is a dedicated corner for us. Immersion my ass.

I clutched my brown paper bag containing leftover Chinese takeout and sat down. I could hear kids snickering as we settled in. They always snicker. This time, the laughter sounded unfortunately familiar. This bothered me more. There was Sarah, Adam (and, oh my Space God, Michaela), and a few others from the Honors crew. Usually they sat by the door. Why were they over here? Adam got up from his table, and Sarah followed. He stood at the head of ours and cleared his throat. Sarah just stood there, looking uncomfortable.

"Hi, guys!" he said brightly. I cocked my head at him.

"What the fuck?" I said out loud. I hadn't meant to. It just sort of slipped out. Bianca, Riley, Greg, and Lance snorted simultaneously. Sarah fidgeted as Adam cleared his throat again.

"Hi! Listen. As you know, my friends and I," he said, gesturing over to Sarah, previously perfect Michaela, and the other Honors goons, "are really working hard on making some changes to the school. Good ones! That can benefit everyone. We really think that with representation on the committee to choose the new school superintendent, the student's voices can be heard."

I sat there, still with my head cocked, still with "WTF" written all over my face. "Go away," I said to the two of them. "You already have your . . . whatever the thing is." I sighed.

"But," Adam continued, ignoring me, "the principal just informed my colleagues and I that a student has been asked to represent us already." Sarah narrowed her eyes at the end of the table. "Without a vote, or anything."

"Listen, dude and Brynn's ex, I don't know what you're talking about. And I really don't care. Do us all a favor. Go away," Bianca said.

I thought I heard Michaela suck in her breath over there at the next table when Bianca said "ex," but I might have imagined it.

"You don't seem to understand," said Adam. "It seems Lacey here is your . . . *our* representative."

All of our heads swiveled toward Lacey. She looked at us, and at Sarah, and Adam. Her hands went to her keyboard. But she just rested them, there, on the keys. She didn't speak.

"And we don't think that's fair," he said. "I mean, for instance, seniors shouldn't be able to—"

"Oh, seniors my ass. This again," I said. "You have something against anyone who isn't you."

Maybe the smell of Adam's cologne was a trigger for me from the last time. I don't know. I was about to stand, when Lacey's voice broke through.

"I didn't ask for it," she said.

"We know," Sarah said.

"And you can turn it down," Adam said flatly. "We know that, too."

"Adam," said Sarah.

"Maybe you *should* turn it down," said Adam. "After all, it'd be a lot of time. And stress. And surely you don't need that." He sounded as if he were talking to a small child.

"Adam, you better . . ." I started to say, but a body stepped in between us before I could continue.

"Hello, Ms. Harper. Mr. Graff. I trust your day is going well?" Mr. Grimm magically appeared on cafeteria duty from his blue room meeting. He's a tall guy. Actually pretty intimidating for a teacher. Adam shrank back.

"Yes, sir, certainly. Just"—Adam looked at our table—"just saying hi." He moved around Mr. Grimm and didn't stop back at his table. He left the cafeteria. Sarah turned and wordlessly followed him. Mr. Grimm looked at me.

"All right, Brynn?" I just nodded. I sank back into my chair. I was just too mad to speak. As I think of it now, all over again, I'm still no less angry. Elitist prick asshole Honors shitheads bother me. I can say this definitively.

Everything else pales in comparison to them. I couldn't even look over at Michaela. *She* was one of *them*.

What would you have done, Rachel? That's my question for you. *What should I have done?*

Lacey left after lunch for a doctor's appointment, and I couldn't talk to her. So I did the only thing I could think of, and went to Sarah's locker after the final bell.

Because I obviously had started liking life too much.

I stood there and I waited. Sarah got there right after I caught my breath from taking the stairs two at a time.

"What?" she asked.

"Why are you helping him?"

"Helping who?" She sighed, opening her locker door.

"You know who." I shoved myself in front of the books she was trying to put away. "You don't like him. You never did. You know he's evil. Or at least too starved to act like a normal person. Why are you doing his bidding?"

"He isn't evil, Brynn. He just doesn't think like you do."

"And how do I think?"

"Listen, the world is what it is. You have to play the game. In order to get good things done, you have to have allies."

"He is not your ally. He is only in stuff for himself. And what good do you want? Why don't you want everyone to have a shot at that superintendent thing? And why are you going after Lacey?"

"This is where you and I disagree, Brynn. No one is going after her. She is out of here at the end of the year. Her interests lie elsewhere—you know it's true. She wants to win the Academic Bowl championship again. She wants to get all the tutoring extra credit to make her the super-uber-valedictorian and then get the hell out of Westing and into the Ivy of her choice. I am concerned about moving forward *here and now*. There needs to be someone motivated who will also be around to see the effects of the superintendent choice. That isn't Lacey, nor is it a lot of the high school population, I'm sad to say."

I moved away. "How would you even know? You talk to seven people."

She shrugged. "Doesn't mean I'm wrong."

"You've changed," I said.

"And you haven't." She tilted her head in my direction. A sad look passed over her eyes. "Sorry, Brynn. Not going to change my mind." She slammed her locker shut. I watched her back until it disappeared down the staircase.

Fuck me for thinking it, but I still wished I were walking next to her. Even if I wouldn't have liked where she was going.

Sincerely,

Brynn

Folder:	Sent
To:	mmaynard@westing.pa.edu
From:	JSG@GraffHunterWexley.net
Date:	October 30
Subject:	Of some concern

Dear Principal Maynard,

It has come to my attention that a student has been asked to fill the spot on the superintendent selection committee. This has caused my wife and I a great deal of confusion. As you are aware, our son Adam, along with many of his classmates, wrote a bill to allow that selection committee spot to be available for a student representative in the first place.

It is categorically unacceptable that this seat would go to a student who was uninvolved in the aforementioned process. My wife and I have tried to instill in Adam a desire to see commitments through to the end. I expect that you will give my concerns all due consideration and find a way to award the selection committee seat to someone with the necessary drive and follow-through to do the best job possible.

Sincerely,

Jonathan S. Graff, Esquire

Folder: Drafts
To: Rachel@msnbc.com
From: Brynnieh0401@gmail.com
Date: October 31
Subject: Questions

Dear Rachel Maddow,

I've been thinking about the question I asked you in the last e-mail. What *would* you have done when King Asshole Adam tried his weird shit with Lacey? I decided to be nice to myself for a change in my answer. Maybe you would have sat there, stunned. Maybe your throat, like mine, would have felt like a bottle full of pennies turned upside down, with nothing able to spill out because the mouth was packed tight. I was all stuck together in that moment. Maybe you are like that sometimes, too. You just have more practice getting unstuck because you are on TV.

Then like the gracious television patronus that you are, you answered my question with your "outrage-o-meter" segment. You asked what it would take to get me so mad that I had to do something. What would have to happen to make me act?

The answer to that, it would seem, is for someone to mess with Lacey.

Today Lacey wasn't herself. She was just sitting quietly in her chair, not really even looking at anything. Even when she's a little under the weather, she still gives us all the evil eye to guilt us into doing our work. This was so disturbing I actually spoke to the traitorous Michaela when she descended into our cave.

"Hey," I whispered.

"Hey," she whispered back, surprised.

"What's with Lacey?"

"What do you mean?"

"She's not harassing anyone about working harder. Or anything."

Michaela cocked her head and raised her eyebrow at me. I shook my head. She didn't know the true ways of Lacey yet. I slid away from

Michaela. But during lunch (in the blue room), I pulled a chair over to Lacey.

"Yo," I said. Nothing. "Laaaacceeyyyyy," I called. "Helloooooo," I said.

She didn't look at me. I looked at her aide, who sighed.

"Lacey. Buddy. You are seriously freaking me out here. What's the matter?" I said.

Lacey's eyes flicked up at me. Her hands moved on her board.

"I'm fine," her voice said.

"You are *not*."

"I'm fine," she said again. I leaned back in my chair and crossed my arms. It's a trick, I'm ashamed to say, I picked up from Fart Weasel.

"Well, if you are fine, then I will just sit here. Staring at you. And we shall both be fine together. Happy Halloween."

Lacey rolled her eyes. This brought me some peace. "Fine," she typed.

"Fine."

"You are seriously annoying."

"Fine."

"Oh my God, Brynn," she said. She typed for a while. "You know what, I wasn't going to tell you this, because I knew what you'd say and I honestly didn't want to have to argue it with you. But you might as well know. I turned down the position on the superintendent selection committee."

It took me a minute to process what she had said. "Oh, Lacey, why?" I asked. "Not because of . . ." I had to take a breath. "Not because of *Adam*?"

"No. Not because of Adam."

"But you are perfect for this! You are the best of all of us. Down here, upstairs. In the whole school. Possibly in the whole of the Earth."

"Brynn, might I . . ." Ms. Yee started.

"Adam is an idiot. And he has *no right* to treat you the way he did, and—"

Lacey's voice interrupted me. "Brynn, it's not about Adam. It really isn't. He's a tool, and I don't care what he or any of the others think. I've told you this a million times. I have enough to do as it is. I don't need to be a poster child for inclusivity or something. Let Adam or Sarah or whoever fight for a school superintendent who will install an Honors lounge on every floor of every school or whatever thing they want. Honestly, I have better things to do with my time. I'm no one's token."

I frowned. A deep seed of unhappiness implanted uncomfortably in my stomach. It was different than the dull ache that I knew well. It was sharp, like a splinter. "But what about us? The Applied people. Or even the Academic people. Or anyone other than Adam. Adam doesn't care about us."

Lacey half shrugged. "True," she said. She glanced up at me and held my gaze. She didn't look outraged. Or upset, even. She looked like she felt bad for *me*.

That made me even angrier. Angry at Adam, at guys like Adam, at Sarah for capitulating to guys like Adam, at all of us sitting in the blue room basically ignored because of . . . what? Circumstance? Fucking circumstance. I seethed my way through English and history and then civics, and the stomach splinter grew and grew until it was a full-on spike through my middle. I could tell everyone was watching me shift in my seat, grind my teeth, ball my hands into fists to keep from freaking out. But my outrage-o-meter was deep in the red.

I was so mad, I ran straight home even though Fart Weasel might have been there (he wasn't). I stopped to kick a tree twice. But as soon as my butt hit my bed, I pulled out my computer and began to type. A thought occurred to me, Rachel. Maybe's it's dumb, but it was a new thought nonetheless. (I can hear Mr. Grimm in my head: "Thoughts are never dumb! They are your brain speaking!")

Even if Lacey doesn't want to do the school board thing, why does King Asshole get to win this one? Maybe the Asshole Kings get what they want most of the time in this life. Does that have to be the case? No. No, it does not. I've seen it on your show. Sometimes the Asshole Kings are taken down because they suck so much they can't hide behind smiles. And sometimes they are put in their place by people who are just outraged enough.

Sincerely,

Brynn

Folder: Drafts
To: Rachel@msnbc.com
From: Brynnieh0401@gmail.com
Date: November 1
Subject: Outraged. Again. Still.

Dear Rachel Maddow,

You are a person who loves your job. Last night you had the House minority whip on. (Hey, the whip helps the party leader get their legislation going on—oh, who knows stuff? Brynnie knows stuff, what what!) And you just looked so joyful on there, even if you were talking about how dysfunctional Congress is and fewer and fewer meaningful bills are passed these days. Maybe with hope comes joy.

Or maybe it's the adrenaline rush of being on live TV.

I'll hope it's both.

My job brings neither joy nor hope, though it does occasionally bring underwear. School, my other job, isn't bringing the joy, either. I tried talking to Mr. Grimm about convincing Lacey to fight for the superintendent selection thing. He gave me a speech about free will and how she'd made up her mind and Ivys were already practically begging her to bring her genius to them already and she didn't need another thing, etc. And then I argued with him and then Lacey again about *what about the rest of us?* I mean, Adam and Sarah are going to get an Honors lounge (that is a real thing that they want, by the way), but the blue room kids have leaky pipes and books where the last whip mentioned is Leslie Cornelius Arends. Do you know when that was, Rachel? Freaking 1975.

Actually, you probably did know that.

Anyway, when I was done, Mr. Grimm got all quiet and looked me up and down like he was sizing me up for a fight. Then all he said was, "That's an interesting point, Brynn. Maybe you should do something about it."

"That's what I'm *trying* to do, Mr. Grimm. But Lacey won't listen to reason." I glared at her.

"This is actually one of the first reasonable things you've said, Brynn." Lacey glared back. "Mostly you operate on emotion."

"So you'll do it?" I asked.

"No. I'm more about art than politics," she said.

"Oh, what does that even *mean*?" I said.

Lacey chuckled. She was so over this whole thing.

"Doesn't anyone think this is wrong? Don't you think all voices should be represented? Don't *we* matter?" My voice was getting higher and more nasal. For a second, I felt like I actually left my body. I hovered over the room and looked at Bianca and Riley.

Mr. Grimm smiled at me. Lacey cocked her head as if in thought. The others clapped.

"There you are, Brynn. Maybe you are the political one of the group," said Mr. Grimm.

"That's impossible," I said.

"Is it?" He raised his eyebrows at me. I did not like how this was going.

"What are you saying?"

"Well, you seem to care about this issue," he said.

I flinched at the word "care." Caring inevitably preceded crushing loss. I learned that after Dad left.

And Nick.

And Sarah.

"And as I recall you have a hero in a political commentator. Maybe you should take action," he said.

He invoked you, Rachel. Oh, no he didn't.

"Yeah. No way. Leave it to the Honors students, then. They have the brains for it." I sulked back to my seat. This was crap, is what it was. I felt stupid for almost giving a damn and guilty because everyone just kept giving me these little side glances the rest of the day.

All of this could have faded away, but then Michaela found me at Aerie at my shift after school that day.

"Hey," she said, coming up to my bins of cotton and lace.

"Oh, hi," I said sarcastically. "Here to peer tutor the bras?" As far as I knew she was still in league with Sarah and Company.

"No. I came for you."

"What?" My face reddened.

"When are you done here?" she asked.

"Um, in like a half an hour?" Not a single snarky reply could come to me.

"Okay. I'll wait. I'll be on the bench." She chucked her thumb toward the entrance and walked away before I could say anything.

I numbly put back all the scattered items until Erin was satisfied. Erin let me go, and sure enough, there was Michaela on the bench, reading a book.

"Lacey is already over all of you and your thing. So don't even worry about it," I blurted.

Michaela sighed. "Listen, Brynn," she said. "I'm still new here. My dad knows Adam's dad, so I met him right before I started. That's why I hung out with them. But . . ." She trailed off. "I was thinking about the thing in the cafeteria. And that maybe it isn't right to exclude any particular group of people from being represented. Which basically is what would happen."

"You want to run for the school board thing?" My heart lifted. Michaela was new, but she was smart. This could work.

She snorted. "Um, no," she said.

My heart sank.

"But *you* should," she said.

"Yeah. No," I said.

"Yeah, *yes*, Brynn."

"There's no way anyone would elect me. I'm a nobody. A blue room nobody at that. And I'm not like a genius candidate like Lacey or anything."

"You are smarter than you let on," Michaela said. "And intelligence has nothing to do with why any of you are down there and you know it."

"Oh, really, now. And you are so sure of this because . . ."

"Because I watch you. I watch everybody. It's a gift of being the new girl. No one notices you, so you can just watch."

"And you watch me?"

"Yes."

"So you think I should, what? Go after the selection committee thingy?"

"Yes. Well, no. Maybe."

"What?" I said.

"What would you really want to happen?"

I narrowed my eyes at her, but my brain clanged against the front of my skull. What I really wanted was to go back to the paper and report the shit out of this. Get the information out to the people. But I wasn't ready to admit that out loud yet.

"I want to punch Adam in the throat," I said.

Michaela shook her head.

I thought about it for another moment. "But I also want to make sure he isn't the one calling all the shots," I said. "Or if he gets to argue for what he wants, that he doesn't make it look like it's what everyone wants. I legit want everyone to get a say. It'd be one thing if teachers or the school board adults were calling the shots, which they pretty much are. But if one student is allowed to try to get stuff, than all the students should get a chance. Even the kids in the rooms named after colors." I nodded forcefully to myself.

"There you go," said Michaela. She smiled and held my pissed-off gaze. "So what are you going to do?"

"Why should I do anything?" I said.

But the ideas were still hammering behind my eyes. The ideas were chanting, "What would Rachel Maddow do? What would Rachel Maddow do?"

Stupid ideas needed to shut their traps.

"For Lacey?" Michaela tried.

"Lacey can take care of herself. Trust me."

"Well then, for you?"

I snorted. "Not gonna lie, I don't really give a shit about me, either."

"Then for the blue room. For the blue roomers to come after you. There will always be an Adam and a Sarah to act like asses. After high school, lots of Adams. Lots of Sarahs. You really want that?"

"Oh my God, who even are you?" I stared at her. It was like she could see the deepest fears buried within my brain.

"I know you try to act like you don't care about anything, but it's obvious you do. You try so hard when you think no one is watching. I like what you said right now. It's cool, Brynn. It's cool that you care. Especially about people no one else cares about. And . . ." She looked down. She opened her mouth like she was going to say something else, but then she didn't.

"And?" I said.

Michaela cleared her throat. "And you should think about it."

"Oh. Okay," I said. Disappointment hit me, though I wasn't entirely sure why. "So what now?" I said.

"You become a freedom fighter," she said. She smiled. She looked at her watch. "Well. Um. I should go. I'll see you?"

"Um. Yeah," I said. I stared, baffled, as she turned suddenly and retreated down the hushed mall corridor. My heart pounded.

What *was* that? Did this mean she liked me? Did I like her?

Yes. Yes, I did like her. Damn it all.

So help me, Rachel Maddow. Is this why people go into politics? Some weird mix of altruism and lust? It is hard to tell which one is more compelling at this point.

Sincerely,

Brynn

Folder: Drafts
To: Rachel@msnbc.com
From: Brynnieh0401@gmail.com
Date: November 2
Subject: Nemesis

Dear Rachel Maddow,

Fridays are usually happy days at school because they mean two days of no class and three evenings of money for Brynn from the sale of underwear. But people can ruin anything, can't they?

I was minding my own business making my way down to my learning cave when Adam literally stepped out of the shadows of the shop wing directly in my path.

"Hi," he said.

I stopped short.

"Adam?" I was too surprised to say or do much else.

"I have a proposition for you," he said.

"No."

"You haven't even heard what it is yet."

"Doesn't matter," I mumbled. I tried to step around him but he maneuvered to my left, and then to my right as I tried to pass him.

"Listen, we can be on the same team here," he said.

"I don't know what you're talking about." I tried to turn around and walk the other way, but dude was too fast and blocked me. "Don't you have to go drink a protein shake and throw some boys around under you or something?"

Adam smiled.

"All right, all right," he said, holding his hands up. "Listen, your peer tutor Michaela seems to think that your ideas about 'equality' and 'all voices being at the table' are worth something. Sarah and I and everyone told her *you* don't give a shit, of course. But she won't listen." His smile faded. "It's a shame. She has potential."

"What does this have to do with me?" I said.

Adam shrugged. "Maybe nothing. I just wanted to say that if we can get Principal Maynard to agree to our proposal, that obviously I . . . or whomever is chosen to help select the next superintendent . . . would be willing to work with all of you."

"Who is this 'you' you keep talking about?" I narrowed my eyes.

"Brynn. Come on. You know. The basement crew."

"Don't—"

"It's where your classroom is located."

"Whatever. No student gets to pick where the classes take place. Listen. I don't know what Michaela said to you, but I just want you to leave me alone. How about that?"

"Fine. Great, actually. Then we have an agreement."

"Fine," I said. Even though we were in the middle of the school hall, I still felt seriously uncomfortable. I moved to walk by him, and he let me go that time.

"It's funny," he said to my back.

I didn't turn.

"Michaela and Sarah get along *really* well. Those two make a great team." He snickered.

My heartbeat picked up.

I didn't stop and look back at him. I wouldn't give him the satisfaction. But Michaela and Sarah were all I could think about for the rest of the day.

Michaela and Sarah, Sarah and Michaela. There's no way that could be a thing.

But still.

Honestly, Rachel, what's a girl even to do?

Sincerely,

Brynn

Folder:	Inbox
To:	Brynnieh0401@gmail.com
From:	justinhmitchell@westing.pa.edu
Date:	November 3
Subject:	You were right!

Dear Brynn,

OMG I think you were right! The contractor in charge of the War Memorial is the mayor's brother-in-law! I think that's why this story died. I found an old op-ed that complained about how the façade was cheap and the materials used were crappy. Bet a lot of people don't want that really getting out there again, right?

That still doesn't say anything about who started the fire. I thought maybe that could implicate someone who wanted to expose the mayor or something, but it's not like he's up for reelection anytime soon. And people love him, so I don't even know if this would matter. Some kids in the journalism room say Adam Graff accidentally caused the fire as part of some prank. Did you hear anything about that?

He'd be in some deep shit if that were true.

It can't possibly be true.

Damn it, Brynn, come back to the paper.

—Justin

Folder:	Drafts
To:	Rachel@msnbc.com
From:	Brynnieh0401@gmail.com
Date:	November 4
Subject:	Thread the needle

Dear Rachel Maddow,

I have been attempting to make things up to Mom, even though I still think it's unfair she won't let me explain what I meant about Nick. If he were an unapproachable subject before, mention of his name is downright cursed now.

"I watered your plants," I said.

"Mm-hmm," she mumbled as she darned Fart Wesel's nasty socks.

"Do you need anything from the store?"

She looked up at me. "Do you want something, Brynn? I don't have much time, and I have a lot to get done."

"I . . ." I said.

Why, yes, Mother dearest. I would appreciate your unconditional love. I'd also settle for maybe you giving a single shit about me every other Thursday.

I didn't say any of that.

What I actually said was, "I'm sorry. For what I said. A while ago. It isn't what I meant."

"Brynn." Her voice threatened tears, just like that.

"I feel like it was my fault he died. Nicky. I thought maybe you did, too. That's all."

She stared at me, hard. No tears.

"Did you give him the drugs?" she said.

"No."

"Neither did I." She went back to darning.

"Okay." I stood there watching her needle, sharp and bright, twinkle in and out of stinky cotton. "So, do you need anything?"

"No," she said. The silver sliver pierced in and out. She didn't look up as I walked past her and left the house to go to the library.

I have to buy my own new socks when the holes in my old ones get too big.

There's only so much time in a day, I guess. You have to pick what's important to you.

Sincerely,

Brynn

Folder: Drafts
To: Rachel@msnbc.com
From: Brynnieh0401@gmail.com
Date: November 6
Subject: Once upon a time

Dear Rachel Maddow,

Today was Sarah's birthday. Last year I put a cupcake in her locker to surprise her. She didn't see it, and before I could say anything, she dropped her math, English, and civics textbooks on top of it. Icing oozed out beneath the bronze bust of a bald eagle.

(Do eagles have busts? Probably. That would explain so much about Aerie's existence, anyway.)

"Ewwwww, Brynnie," she yelled at me.

"I was trying to be romantic!" I said. "You said you liked romance."

"I meant that I wanted you to buy me a necklace or something! Maybe go out to Red Lobster!"

"Why didn't you just say that? Then I wouldn't have tried to get creative."

Sarah shook her head, exasperated. She picked up her books and handed the top two to me. She surveyed the damage to *Problems of Democracy*. "Eh," she said. "Only a little bit sticky." She looked at me, a familiar fiendish glint in her eye. "No harm done." She licked the icing off the book.

"Ewwwww, where has that book *been*?" I said, my turn to be disgusted.

"Probably nowhere stranger than my mouth." She grabbed me and pulled me into a kiss.

"Ugh. Desk germs. Backpack germs." I shoved her away.

She laughed and gathered up the smashed crumbs. "Thank you for the birthday present."

Her parents got her a gift card to Red Lobster, so she ended up getting part of her romantic birthday anyway.

This year I thought about trying the same thing. But she probably had someone else she wanted to be with. Someone who would know not to ruin her books and would get her a necklace.

Someone better than me.

Sincerely,

Brynn

Folder: Drafts
To: Rachel@msnbc.com
From: Brynnieh0401@gmail.com
Date: November 9
Subject: Up all night

Dear Rachel Maddow,

You often say that you won't be getting any sleep. Is that true? It must be, because you are a reporter and reporters have to tell the truth. How do you function, then? Maybe you just mean you stay at work really late?

I had continued thinking about my unfortunate encounter with Adam since it happened. Everything about it bothered me. I just thought and thought. I went over to Leigh and Erin's for dinner, and even though we were getting burritos, it still bothered me.

"Someone fucking with you, kid?" Leigh had asked. He doesn't talk much, so I must have looked pretty upset.

"Do you know anything about politics?" I asked him. He rolled a cigarette and went off about legalized marijuana until Erin brought home the food and he forgot what we had been talking about in the first place.

At school, I ignored Michaela completely when she came in. She came over twice and asked me if I wanted to talk about the math. I just shook my head. At lunch, Lacey rolled over.

"You okay?"

"Yup. Fine."

"You don't look okay."

"I'm fine, Lacey."

"Is this about me? Because honestly—"

"No, it's not," I stopped her. I shook my head. "It's not."

"Well, good. But it must be something. Are you mad at Michaela? Because I think she likes you."

I stared down at my ham sandwich. I mashed a corner of it with my thumb.

"So it is about her?"

"Lacey, can we not talk about this?"

She sat there for a while, not saying anything. I refused to look up at her.

"Fine, Brynn. But here's something I've learned. A piece of advice from me to you."

I flicked my eyes to hers.

"If you want something, really want something, you have to fight for it."

I grunted. She sighed and left me alone.

However, Rachel, just now on your show, you were talking to a senator from Illinois. Or Indiana. One of the "I" states, I wasn't really paying attention. Anyway, you were talking about campaign reform and sustainable architecture and smart things, and you asked the senator about her campaign. And she said, "Well, Rachel. I've learned that if you want something, really want something, you have to fight for it. But sometimes it takes a while to figure out what the people really want."

It was a message from the universe. Lacey was right. That senator from Indiana or possibly Illinois or Idaho was right. If you really want something, you have to act.

But what would that look like?

Watch this space.

Your fan,

Brynn

Folder: Drafts
To: Rachel@msnbc.com
From: Brynnieh0401@gmail.com
Date: November 12
Subject: 366 days, but who is counting?

Dear Rachel Maddow,

Justin talked me into getting coffee with him since we had the day off of school.

"In about a year from now, we will be able to vote!" Justin enthused into his latte.

"More like five months for me," I said.

"You could help elect way more women! Into the Senate or House or for local down-ticket races. Who knows, the White House could be in play again."

"Yes." I sipped the venti that Justin had purchased to bribe me into being seen in a known Honors hangout.

"Aren't you excited about that?"

"Well," I sighed. "Honestly, I think a woman, any woman, is going to have a hard time getting elected. I'm convinced districts and counties and states will pick any insane blowhard dude over a woman almost every time."

"That is a really cynical way to look at it."

I shrugged. "Or just realistic."

"Well then, we just need more women to run. It's a numbers game. The people need to hear the right voice at the right time. And that voice is just as likely to be a woman."

"Yeah." I sighed again. "One can hope for more people like that. Real-deal public servants."

"That would be awesome," Justin said. "The world needs more public servants."

"Yup," I said.

We sat there and sipped our coffee. A year from now. Where would I be? Where do I want to be? I could vote next year. But maybe there were things to do on a more minor level now.

Sincerely,

Brynn

Folder: Drafts
To: Rachel@msnbc.com
From: Brynnieh0401@gmail.com
Date: November 13
Subject: Super Tuesday

Dear Rachel Maddow,

I woke up today a new woman. Newish. A little newer. Well, okay. Maybe I was the same old woman, but I felt a fire surging around inside my body like some sort of alien from one of those movies Nick used to make me watch.

Erin picked me up and gave me a ride to school. "You okay there?" she said. "You're breathing funny. Like you are going to have an asthma attack. You got asthma?"

"No. I have a mission."

"You still going to show up for your shift?"

"Yeah."

"Well, go get 'em, kid." Erin shifted into park for two seconds while I threw myself out of the car.

I went straight to the principal's office. I elbowed my way through the locker doors and sea of hoodies and coats. I thrust myself into the narrow room that was too quiet compared to outside. Esther, the secretary, looked up at me. We knew each other from antics past, like when I had been kicked out of English class for pointing out the teacher was a fascist.

Four or five times.

I maintain the truth of that claim.

"Well, hello, Ms. Harper. It's been a while. You don't have an appointment?"

I sniffed a little. "No. But could I please see Principal Maynard?"

A head popped out of his office then. "Well, hello, Ms. Harper," said Maynard himself. "You are here to see me . . . voluntarily?"

I sniffed again. "Um. Yes, sir?"

"Well, come on in." He gestured grandly to his office, like this was a big favor.

I kind of wanted to hate him, but he'd never been too much of an asshat, given the things ~~Nick~~ us Harpers had done at Westing High over the years.

"I was reviewing budgets for a football boosters meeting later. I hate the budget. I was afraid I would have to stare at spreadsheets all morning." He looked at me. "So."

I cleared my throat. "Yeah. Okay. I was wondering . . ."

Oh man. I was in way over my head. Oh man, oh man. I should get out now. What was I even *doing*? I didn't care about shit. No, wait. Get it together, Brynn. I thought of you, Rachel. I prayed that somewhere, deep down inside, there was an inner activist waiting to be unleashed.

"Okay," I started again. "This superintendent thing. You know how there can be a student on the committee thingy who selects him? Or her."

"Yes?" Mr. Maynard raised his eyebrows. "There was quite a bit of lobbying to change the law on that. Failed in the state senate a few times. Politics." He sighed and shook his head.

"But it's law now."

"Yes."

"And the school gets to pick the student who sits on the committee?"

Again he raised his eyebrows. "Well, that is up for some debate." He chuckled. "The law didn't specify that per se. It's kind of a loose policy at the moment. We are working on defining that. Some of your fellow students are trying to shape that policy, as you may know."

"Yes. I do," I said, trying to keep the venom out of my voice.

"The vice principal and I were going to pick a student. We did pick one, actually. But she turned us down. Some members of Student Government were thus adamant that they get to pick their representative."

"But their petition is to get an *Honors* student to be the representative."

"Well, yes. Their logic for that was compelling."

"But that logic is *flawed*." Now I was going all Mr. Grimm on him. "Why should these twenty or thirty people have some sort of advantage over hundreds? Shouldn't *anyone* be allowed to be a candidate? Isn't that *American*?"

You know, I don't know if it's American. Can anyone run for public office? What if you did a turn in juvie? But I swear, Rachel, all the stuff you talk about makes it seem like democracy means everyone has a voice. Or some shit like that.

"Well." I could see Mr. Maynard regarding me. "I see where you are coming from. No one made that argument."

"I am. I am making that argument. If Lacey won't do it, *which she totally should because she is awesome and I respect you for seeing that, Mr. Maynard*, then anyone who cares enough should be given a chance." I banged my fist on his desk. A marble from a little pyramid puzzle rolled away. Mr. Maynard caught it with one fluid motion. Dude was some sort of fucking ninja principal.

"I see," was all he said.

I think both of us were surprised that I was making something out of this.

"Do you want a chance?" he asked. "To be on the superintendent selection committee?"

"No," I admitted. "No. But I'm in the blue room, you know. Applied. And not far from the red-room freshman and yellow-room sophomores and the green-room seniors . . ." I sighed. "Nobody cares about us down there."

Mr. Maynard opened his mouth. I raised my hands.

"I mean, none of the kids here. Especially Honors and Student Government and those types." I knew this *intimately*, but I couldn't tell him that. "And maybe whoever is picked won't, either. But there are as many of us down there with opinions as there are Honors kids. And there's a whole lot more shop kids, or academic athletes, or whatever.

•

And there are smart people who consider themselves parts of lots of groups, or no group at all!"

Holy balls. I hoped he went for this because, honest to Hayes, I had used pretty much every thought my brain had to offer at this point. Fortunately he started nodding.

"Okay, Brynn," he said. "I hear you. But I'll tell you—you are in fact the only other student who came in here about this. No one else has been banging down the door to represent the study body in picking a superintendent. Tell you what. Craft me a statement, telling me why you think there should be a runoff for the superintendent selection committee seat."

Why do adults do this? You show a shred of interest in something, and they have to slaughter the good thing by assigning more work? He's the damn principal; can't he just change the rules? But I'd been all passionate and shit about democracy five minutes ago.

"Make sure you clearly state what you want to see happen," Maynard said, pointing at me. He smiled again. "Good luck."

I grunted something in reply. I was annoyed by how pleased he looked. Or maybe just a little confused. Can't say I'd ever gotten that kind of reaction from his office before. It either meant that I was doing the right thing, or setting myself up for disaster.

Watch this space.

Sincerely,
Brynn

Folder: Drafts
To: Rachel@msnbc.com
From: Brynnieh0401@gmail.com
Date: November 14
Subject: And I'll write your name

Dear Rachel Maddow,

Erin and Leigh play the "bad news, good news" game. If you have bad news and good news, you always give the bad news first. Like, Leigh will say, "Hey, the bad news is my car got towed, but I gave the guy at the impound lot a blow job—yes, I was safe—so the good news is that I didn't have to pay the hundred-fifty bucks!" That's a bad example, but you get what I'm saying.

The bad news is that I got my grades for the first quarter. Mr. Grimm gave me a B, the first B I've gotten in years, mostly because he knows I write to you all the time. Even if my essays and tests still kind of suck, I am getting extra credit. And he doesn't even read this shit! Ha! He also teaches civics and history, blue room being what it is and all. And I got two Cs and another B. But I got a D in math. I can't afford Ds. I won't have the GPA to get back on the paper (or maybe one day graduate?) with Ds. Ms. Yee is upset with me. I know she is. Teachers really hate it when they think you can do it and then you don't.

There *is* a person, you might be thinking, who could *peer tutor* me in, say, math and science.

(We'll just stick a pin in that thought for now.)

On the other hand, the good news is the whole statement for the superintendent selection committee. The blue room practically exploded when I announced what happened with Mr. Maynard yesterday.

"You did something. You actually did something," said Lacey. "Go, Brynn."

"Yeah, who are you?" said Bianca. She giggled. I'm pretty sure she thought I was joking.

"I need to craft a statement!" I declared. "Lacey, craft me a statement."

"Bite me," she said.

"Riley? Greg?" I said, turning to them, hoping to affect something approaching charm.

"You are going to have to do this, Brynn. It was your idea." Bianca shook her head at me. "But we will help?" she said, glancing around the room.

Mr. Grimm looked positively ecstatic.

"This *is* civics!" he declared, a massive grin on his face.

All of this positive attention in school was making me a little nauseous. With everyone's input (everyone being mostly Mr. Grimm and Lacey), my statement was simple. It read, "We the students of Westing High School would like to make it the school policy to run a whole school election each year necessary to determine the student representative on the superintendent selection committee."

"Elegant," said Mr. Grimm. He even offered to print it out and turn it in to Mr. Maynard's office himself.

That was pretty much the highest praise possible from him.

Sincerely,
Brynn

Folder: Drafts
To: Rachel@msnbc.com
From: Brynnieh0401@gmail.com
Date: November 15
Subject: So here's a thing

Dear Rachel Maddow,

The last forty-eight hours or so have been amazing. I worried that maybe Mr. Maynard was going to ignore me, but he didn't. He made *photocopies*. And he took them to his meeting. And it went over really well. He told me this afternoon, and I smiled for the rest of the day.

But today my buzz was slashed into tiny pieces. I was on my way to blue room when Sarah and Adam met me by the stairs.

"Yes?" I asked. My heart pounded. There was no way this was good.

"You dirty, underhanded little . . ." he started.

"Whoa, Adam. Not cool," Sarah said. She glared at him. "What he means to say, Brynn"—Sarah glared at Adam again—"is that we heard about your underhanded trick. That wasn't cool, either."

"What underhanded trick?" I asked.

"You went behind our backs because you were pissed Lacey decided not to do the superintendent thing. *Her* choice, by the way. So you went to the principal and then you somehow talked Mr. Maynard into thinking we need a runoff for the superintendent selection committee seat."

"Whoa. I didn't go behind your backs. I told you to your face that the whole 'only who Honors people want to pick' shit was wrong. So I talked to the principal, like anybody can. And he told me to convince him. So I did."

Amusement or surprise or maybe even pride passed over Sarah's face for a split second. I knew every twitch of her face so well I could see it, even if Adam didn't.

"You mean to tell me you went and wrote something in like ten seconds and convinced Maynard and the rest of the selection committee. Just like that?" Adam spat. "Like they'd listen to you."

"Funny thing, Adam. They did indeed. This whole thing is legit," I said. I tried to get around him, but he stopped me. It was no wonder the guy was a freaking all-state wrestler, because there was no outmaneuvering him.

"Fine," Sarah said, her lips back into their typical thin line. "Fine, then. A whole-school runoff it is. Whoever gets the most votes will be the voice of the people, fair and square."

Adam narrowed his eyes for a second, like he was thinking. A smile spread across his face. "Yes." He grinned. "The *popular* vote *is* the will of the people."

Heat crept into my cheeks. An icky feeling followed it. Of course they had the fucking advantage. God I was stupid. Who would go up against them?

"Thank you, Brynn," said Adam. "I guess this is for the best. You would know and all." Sarah looked at him warily, like even she was afraid of what he was thinking. He turned and walked down the hall. Sarah's gaze lingered on me for a second, her eyes filled again with a look I had longed to see for months. She leaned over a little as if to whisper something to me, but then she must have changed her mind. She leaned back, considered me for a second longer, and turned and followed Adam.

I got the distinct feeling things weren't going to be amazing again for quite some time.

Sincerely,

Brynn

Folder:	Sent
To:	mmaynard@westing.pa.edu
From:	JSG@GraffHunterWexley.net
Date:	November 15
Subject:	Follow-up

Dear Principal Maynard,

Thank you for the productive conversation. I now understand the reasoning behind how the superintendent selection committee seat will be determined for students. I am confident that the outcome will be one we will all find acceptable. I would hope that all relevant parties would be allowed *plenty of time* to state their case to the "voters."

You will also be hearing from several contacts of mine concerning donations addressing some of the school's technological deficits. I am happy to do my part for my alma mater.

Sincerely,

Jonathan S. Graff, Esquire

Folder:	Drafts
To:	Rachel@msnbc.com
From:	Brynnieh0401@gmail.com
Date:	November 16
Subject:	Days off

Dear Rachel Maddow,

It's downright distressing when you are not on your show. It's a little less distressing now. Now I might be at work or I can bug Erin or whatever. But still. I depend on you. Thanksgiving is coming, and I know you'll be off fishing or relaxing for days then. *Days*, Rachel. I guess I'll just listen to *Drift* to tide me over.

Today was far from relaxing. Mr. Maynard actually came down to the blue room to find me.

"Ahem." We heard someone clear his throat from the blue threshold. "Hello, students," said Mr. Maynard awkwardly. "Brynn, may I have a word with you?"

I looked over to Ms. Yee. It's not like I should really be leaving the rocks and minerals lecture. On the other hand, the principal was standing right there. She shrugged her consent. I glanced at Lacey, who I think threw a subtle thumbs-up at me. I followed Mr. Maynard into the hall.

"Brynn, I wanted to let you know how impressed we all were with your dedication. Your argument was thoughtful, concise, and so quickly executed. You have a way with words."

If by "a way with words," he meant "that statement was nice, but you still aren't allowed back on the paper," then sure.

He cleared his throat. "I wanted to let you know that we wanted to hold elections before winter break, since the spring gets into Student Government elections and all. So the runoff vote for the superintendent seat will be held the day before we leave for winter break."

"Sure, Mr. Maynard, okay."

"You and Mr. Graff can begin to organize accordingly."

"Wait, what?" I said. "*Me* and Mr. Graff?" I was annoyed Adam and I were in the same sentence. "I told you I wasn't going to try for the spot. I just thought . . . you know . . . others might like the chance."

Mr. Maynard's smile faltered. "I see." He rubbed his chin. "Well, I guess we'll see if any other of your fellow students step up by Wednesday."

"Okay," I said.

I went back to the blue room, and I tried to pay attention. At the end of the day, we were called to a school assembly. The pep band played. The cheerleaders cheered. Ms. Suarez, the vice principal, gave a speech about civic engagement and what a superintendent does. She encouraged us that if anyone wanted to help pick one they could participate in the runoff to win the committee seat. There was a lot of cheering. I put my face in my hands in the back row. At least my name was not mentioned.

Afterward, feeling desperate, I physically threw myself in front of Lacey. "Lacey, oh my God," I said.

"What?" She looked at me like I had three heads.

"You have to run. You have to. Bianca. Riley. Lance. Greg, tell her she has to run."

"Brynn, she'd be running for a thing she could have had with no effort at all," Lance said.

I glared at him. "Lacey, you must know some high-achieving people from this school. They can do it."

"I"—pause—"do." Pause, pause. "They are afraid of the guy who wants the seat." Click, click. "But I will help you"—buttons—"when you realize you are the only other one."

"Only other one what?" I said.

Lacey rammed into me, and I moved. The look on her face clearly stated that she was over this conversation.

"Only one what?" I asked out loud to no one in particular.

"Don't you pay attention, Brynn?" Bianca said. "Only one who wants to help select the next superintendent!"

"No way." I shook my head vigorously at her. "You know those lean and hungry Student Government types. They live for this. Making the world a better place and shit. There will be five people signed up to try for the spot on that selection committee in a day. I'm not worried."

Lacey gave her skeptical chuckle.

Trust me, Rachel. I know these people. Lots of them will step up. You'll be back on the air tomorrow, a bunch of people who know that Adam is a tool will try for the seat, all will be fine. Yes. I'm totally sure of it.

Sincerely,

Brynn

Folder:	Drafts
To:	Rachel@msnbc.com
From:	Brynnieh0401@gmail.com
Date:	November 19
Subject:	Wrong

Dear Rachel Maddow,

Well, shit. I was wrong. Wrong, wrong, wrong. So complete was my wrongness that I have stomach cramps thinking about it. Maynard and Suarez, Principals of Doom, gave everyone a deadline to try for the superintendent selection seat by November 21, the day before break. All you had to do was put your name on a list to be considered. But Lacey's aide heard in the office that no one had yet stepped up. Right now it was just Adam who wanted it. He must have known it, too, because the smug that surrounded his body was so thick you couldn't even see the loser twat.

No. He defiles the good name of twats everywhere. Dude is a douchebag. No, wait. Actually, I've never noticed before, but all these insults have to do with the lady business. What's with that? Adam is a slime mold ball sack.

There. I feel better.

Unfortunately, people apparently like slime mold ball sacks, because they don't want to go up against him. Or at least the fifteen people I tried to talk into running against him sure didn't.

"Dude," I said to Rick, a yellow roomer, in art. "Don't you want to make a difference? Don't you want to *engage*?"

"I'd like to *engage* with Bianca." He looked over at her and she snorted. "Do you think you can make that happen?"

She flipped him off.

I rolled my eyes. "I don't think you are taking this seriously. So no. I will not campaign for you to get in Bianca's pants."

Everyone was like that. Maybe they didn't want to fuck Bianca (though several did—she gagged at the idea of high school boys), but they all had their own thing. Post-season. Pre-season. Scrapbooking. Probation. I heard it all.

"Honestly, I don't get it," I told Erin while I helped her rip open the flats of new underwear at work. "How does no one *care*?"

Erin took a box cutter to a flat. She sliced it with a deft, almost scary efficiency. "Because people don't, Brynn. Not really. Until they do."

I looked at her.

"I'm serious. Caring for caring's sake isn't typical. People only start to care when something affects *them* personally."

"But this *does* affect them! The superintendent makes decisions that will affect stuff at school for *years*. They could have a voice! A small one maybe, but still." I picked up a stack of bras.

"Maybe. But that's hard to see. Only if something hurts them or makes them sad or pisses them off does it really sink it. And this new-superintendent thing seems far removed from their everyday lives. Probably won't even meet the guy."

"Or woman," I said.

"Or woman," she added. "And I know this person could make policies that will make life worse little by little, or even by a lot for students. And *then* maybe students will complain and say it's so unfair that somebody somewhere did this. And *then*, if you're lucky, maybe they'll realize that they could have done something, but didn't, so it's kinda on them."

Slash went the box cutter.

I stared at her. That was so . . . not what I wanted to hear. It was like a bad day on your show, when the bad news piled up.

"Well. There are a few more days. Maybe someone will step up," I said.

"Maybe," Erin said. She didn't look convinced.

It'll work out. Someone will go against Adam who won't be me, and all will be well. Seriously. I'm 100 percent sure.

90 percent sure. 85 percent at the least.

Sincerely,

Brynn

Folder: Drafts
To: Rachel@msnbc.com
From: Brynnieh0401@gmail.com
Date: November 20
Subject: Here goes nothing

Dear Rachel Maddow,

Since things seem to be taking a turn toward Brynn the Involved again, I had to take drastic steps. My heart lived in the journalism room, or at least it did when it maintained a 2.3 GPA. So I needed to do what needed to be done to get back there.

"Hello, Michaela. Might I speak with you, please?" I said when a certain curly-haired peer tutor arrived in my study hall.

"Sure, Brynn," she said. "What's up?"

"I need to get my grades up more. Like, yesterday."

"Okay?"

"So maybe you can tutor me. Like, a lot."

"Okay? I am here five times a week already, you know. I'm pretty sure Lacey doesn't like me on her turf. Apparently I confused Lance. She basically said I should only work with you."

Of course Lacey did. Freaking Lacey.

"Good. So, will you help me?" I kind of choked on my words.

"Sure." She smiled.

"After school?"

"Sure."

"How about in the evenings?"

"Uh . . ."

"Will you go out with me?" I blurted.

My brain was trying to shut my mouth, but my mouth had terminated its connection and was operating independently.

"Wait. Are you asking me out or asking for help with school work?"

"Both." I shook my head in horror at myself. "Both. See, it's the responsibility of the free press to inform people so that they can elect civically minded representatives! But I need higher grades for that. I still need a two-point-three to be on the paper, and idiot blowhards will win elections unless we try really hard." I slumped in my desk, basically just puking words at that point.

After a moment, Michaela said, "I'd go out with you, you know. Even if the fate of the free press or our democracy or whatever weren't at stake."

"Really?"

"Yes." Michaela smiled. "And I'd be happy to help you with school stuff."

"Oh. Well, good, then. I really do need the help," I said.

"Okay," she said. She wrote her number on an index card and handed it to me.

"Okay."

It was a sweet moment, Rachel. I don't know if I'm helping the sisterhood advance in journalism or politics or not, but a girl can dream.

Sincerely,

Brynn

Folder: Drafts
To: Rachel@msnbc.com
From: Brynnieh0401@gmail.com
Date: November 21
Subject: 5:01 pm

Dear Rachel Maddow,

I stayed at school under the pretense of getting extra-credit assignments from Ms. Yee. And I did visit her briefly. But the minutes ticked by and I couldn't stand it anymore. I went to the principal's office.

"Ah, Brynn, nothing like a deadline, huh?" Mr. Maynard greeted me as I walked in. He was standing at the secretary's desk, collating. He smiled. "Esther is off today, traveling to see her family in Oregon. I couldn't figure out how to get the copier to do this. I'm just finishing up."

"Ah," I said.

"Do you have something you'd like to tell me?"

"Um. Well, I was wondering if anyone decided to try. For the seat. To select the superintendent."

"Just Mr. Graff."

"Seriously, though. Just him?"

"Just him." His eyes shone. "Couple of kids asked about it, but decided not to go for it." He shrugged.

I was a blue roomer. He was supposed to ignore me until I went away. What the actual fuck? "Well. Then." I cleared my throat. I fiddled with the lint in my coat pocket. I felt hot and cold all at the same time. "Then I would like to try for it. Too. For the seat. New superintendent, you know." I was starting to babble. "I'm running. I'm getting extra help with schoolwork because I know there is a grade requirement for this sort of thing. For holding office."

I had to do it. Adam was slimy. He'd ooze all over the committee and probably help them pick a school superintendent as slimy as he was. Even if he didn't have any power, he'd find a way to make sure he came out ahead. That's what slimy ball sack Adam always managed to do.

"Excellent. Have a great Thanksgiving, Brynn."

I nodded. I walked out into the chill afternoon, twilight already settling around me.

So there it is, Rachel. I'm running. Against Adam.

Representative democracy help us all.

Sincerely,

Brynn

Folder: . Drafts
To: Rachel@msnbc.com
From: Brynnieh0401@gmail.com
Date: November 22
Subject: Giving Thanks

Dear Rachel Maddow,

On Wednesday night, Mom texted me from inside the house and said that I had better be at home for Thanksgiving dinner. This was not cool. I protested, saying I had to work Black Friday prep, but Mom said that we needed to have dinner together as a "family."

I do not think that word means what she thinks it means.

So I was crushed around the saddest wooden table in the world, my knees practically touching Fart Weasel, the smell of his body odor matching the rank turkey. I breathed through my mouth for the eternity of their company. Fart Weasel got on me about grades, and Mom got on me about applying to college.

"Mom, that's probably not in the cards for me, you know," I said. I wasn't even trying to be a dick. It was just the truth.

"Brynn, you need to consider your future," she said.

When did she start caring again about my future? Or my present or past, for that matter.

"You ain't staying here, kid, when you turn eighteen. You've had a free ride with a nice room and board and shit, and your momma doesn't make you pay for nothin'. This gravy train is ending!"

The man likely knew a lot about gravy, I'll give him that.

"Okay," I said through clenching teeth.

You know when people say their blood started boiling? Does that actually happen? Is that an actual medical condition, or did someone just make that up? Remind me to do an Internet search for that, Rachel. Because it felt like my skin was starting to get a hot, prickling kind of sensation all over.

"Okay? That's all you got to say, girl?"

"Yeah."

Fart Weasel never had had much to say to me, in all these years. But whenever he did, I found it best not to engage.

"You are so stupid. Stupid and lazy. Just like your brother and just like your daddy. Your momma works so hard. How she ended up with you two shits I don't know."

"Funny. I wondered the same thing about you," I said. I clenched my teeth together so hard I thought one might crack.

Heat began to bubble just under my skin's surface. In two seconds flat, it was practically steaming out of my pores.

Keep it cool, Brynn. Keep it cool, I kept thinking. But he brought up Nick.

"Brynn! You apologize to your father!"

"*He's* not here," I said pointedly. "If you are referring to *that*"—I jutted my chin at Fart Weasel—"he can kiss my ass."

I didn't even see his hand coming. I'd never seen Fart Weasel violent before, even with Nick. He slapped me so hard, I fell backward in my flimsy chair and lay there on the floor for a few seconds, seeing stars. I gingerly touched my face. A little streak of blood from my nose pooled on my fingertip. I was too surprised to be in pain yet.

"Get. The fuck. Out," bellowed Fart Weasel.

Mom now said nothing, but I could see through my own blurry eyes that she was crying. Red-faced, snot-nosed, bawling, in fact. Still mostly in shock, my brain wondered if he had ever hit her, and I'd just never been around or cared enough to notice.

"Out! I said out!" he screamed again. "See how you like it out on the streets!"

This time I got up and stumbled toward the door. I had on the one good pair of boots I owned already on, and I grabbed my coat on my way out.

I clutched my coat around me as the wind whipped my hair around. The bitter air stung and called attention to my face, which fucking hurt.

It seemed to take twice as long to walk to Leigh and Erin's place. It was dark and some of the back roads weren't lit at all. My phone was dead, so I couldn't even use that for light.

When I got to Leigh and Erin's, I spilled through their door and landed in a heap next to the coat closet.

"Brynn?" I heard Erin call from the couch. "That you?" I didn't get up right away.

"Did you hitch a ride over here on the back of a semi or something?" Leigh said.

"You okay?" Erin came over to me and lifted my chin to get a better look at my face.

My brain wasn't working correctly. I couldn't speak. I was too cold, and too dazed.

"My God, Brynn, what the hell happened? Who did this to you?"

Leigh came over then, and the two of them hoisted me up to my feet. I could only just keep shaking my head. The pain was real now, my nose and cheek throbbing. Then everything started shaking. They kind of dragged me over to a chair. Erin got me some Tylenol and some frozen peas wrapped in a towel. She handed the peas to Leigh, who sat on a chair arm and held them to my face.

"Ouch!" I said.

"Oh, thank God. You can speak," Erin said.

"Yeah."

"You get in a bar fight, kid?" asked Leigh.

"Something like that," I said.

"Cool," said Leigh, though I don't think he meant it.

I flinched as he adjusted the ice. "Actually, I'm my stepfather's new favorite punching bag."

"Motherfucker," said Leigh sympathetically. He raised his beer in salute to me. "Whatever you need, kid."

"You should press charges," said Erin half-heartedly. She knew I wouldn't do that. The police in Westing knew the name Harper too well, and Fart Weasel had buddies at the station.

"Brynn, why don't you sleep here tonight? Did you eat?" asked Erin.

The memory of Mom's "turkey" puked all over my brain. I shuddered a little. "I'm not hungry. Thanks, though." I started to get up. "I must look pretty pathetic," I said.

"Nah, you're badass," said Erin. "And you still got all your teeth. You're fine."

"Motherfuckers." Leigh raised his beer to me again.

I nodded at them and followed Erin to their spare bedroom. The throbbing turned to a dull ache, and I fell asleep thinking of ways I could harm Fart Weasel's car. I hated the idea of going home again. But that house had never been a home to begin with, so maybe I wasn't really? It was a holding pen until I turned eighteen. But at least at the moment I was somewhere safe, where no one hated me.

And if I'm being totally honest, Rachel, it wasn't the worst Thanksgiving I've ever had.

Sincerely,
Brynn

Folder:	Drafts
To:	Rachel@msnbc.com
From:	Brynnieh0401@gmail.com
Date:	November 23
Subject:	Black Friday

Dear Rachel Maddow,

I woke up to find Erin standing over my bed.

"I'm not trying to be creepy, but Margie called in sick and it's Black Friday, Brynn. Is your eye swollen shut?"

I blinked against the dim light coming through the curtains. I touched my face. "No, I don't think so."

"Good. Come work. Work is good for the soul."

Since I was a guest, I figured I should listen to her.

"I've seen worse from the dentist," said Leigh. I think he meant the bruise that had formed over night.

Fortunately, Erin was able to hide everything with makeup. I felt painted, but if painted added to the funds that would get me out of Mom and Fart Weasel's den of dickheadedness, then I was ready to sacrifice for the cause.

The mall was swarmed by ten in the morning, and I ran around like a chicken with her head chopped off by her stepfather all day. Afterward I went back to Erin and Leigh's place. I had about fifteen texts and three calls from Mom.

"You shouldn't have spoken to him like that," one said.

"You do this to yourself," said another.

"Why do you do this to me?" said another.

"Are you fucking dead?"

"I'm not dead," I typed.

I watched the little dots of her reply blink on and then disappear. Blink, vanish, blink, vanish. Finally, one word. "Okay."

That was it.

I lay in Erin and Leigh's warm, comfortable extra bed. I stared at the chipping paint on the ceiling. It occurred to me that Nick might have stayed in this exact place. In this same bed. I rolled my face onto the pillow and flinched as my bruised face brushed against a scratchy, faded rose. I longed to smell his cologne one more time. But the comforter just smelled like detergent.

Oh, Nick. How did you get here, cracked and broken like old coats of primer? How did I? I was lost. But I was also warm, and cared for. I bet Nick was, too, when he came here.

Why wasn't this enough?

Sincerely,

Brynn

Folder: Drafts
To: Rachel@msnbc.com
From: Brynnieh0401@gmail.com
Date: November 25
Subject: Homeward Bound

Dear Rachel Maddow,

Did you ever work retail? You did yard work. I read that somewhere. Maybe I should get into yard work.

After Mom sent me another ten texts, I told Erin I should probably go home before the police showed up at her place. She wasn't a fan of the idea, but she also didn't offer to adopt me.

I got back to the Castle Fart while Mom and Weasel were still at church. I spotted a pie in the refrigerator that I desperately wanted to down, but the risk was too great.

I heard the front door squeak open.

I walked into the living room. Fart Weasel narrowed his eyes at me, squinting together thoughts of I don't know what.

"Clean the bathroom," Mom said.

I didn't answer. I just got bleach and a sponge and the toilet bowl brush from under the kitchen sink. They watched me go to the bathroom.

I thought about opening the window and letting in a chipmunk or pigeon or animal helper friend like Cinderella. But I was fresh out of magic, and my face still hurt like a motherfucker. I'd probably scare off any woodland creature worth its weight in cleaning products.

Sincerely,

Brynn

Folder: Drafts
To: Rachel@msnbc.com
From: Brynnieh0401@gmail.com
Date: November 26
Subject: Are you my mother?

Dear Rachel Maddow,

Mom and Fart Weasel returned to the "ignore Brynn completely unless they want her to do something" brand of parenting. I left the house when Mom left the house as often as I could. I didn't know if she really offered any measure of protection from the thing she married, but part of me hoped she did.

Eventually I got tired of only having Erin to talk to. I texted Lacey, but she had challenged her grandfather to a chess tournament and it had expanded to include several brackets of family members. So I did something dangerous.

"Hey," I texted Michaela. "It's Brynn."

"Hi! How was your Thanksgiving?"

"Long story."

"Oh."

I stared at the phone.

"You asked me out," she texted.

"I did."

"Want me to come over?" she said.

"That's probably not the best plan. I could come over to your place."

"That's probably not the best plan, either. How about the mall?"

"God, no."

"Right! Okay, library?"

"Now you're talking."

We met at the big stone lion at the front entrance and found a spot in the back between the kids' and teens' sections.

"I brought homework," I said. I hadn't meant to, it was already in my backpack. But it seemed like a good icebreaker.

"Oh! Okay. What do you want to work on?"

"I don't," I said.

She laughed. She looked at me. "What happened to your face?"

"I . . ." I couldn't think of a plausible excuse. Nothing came to mind. "My mom married someone terrible, and I mention that to him from time to time. He . . ." I stopped for a second. "This was the first time he hit me."

"Wow. That . . ." She stopped. I could see her trying to think of the right words. I knew there weren't really any good ones. "That really sucks. Does it hurt?"

"Kinda."

She moved her puffy chair closer to mine. "He really doesn't do that that often?"

"No. I'm hoping it's not his new thing. Mostly he just quietly loathes me from a separate location."

"Why does he loathe you?"

I considered that. "I hated him first?"

Michaela shook her head. "Oh, Brynn."

"He might hate me because he thinks I'm like my brother," I said. Before Michaela said anything else, I just started telling her Nick's life story. She looked at all of the stupid pictures I had saved on my phone. Even the shots I'd snapped as copies of the Polaroids of him as a toddler. "He was so smart and funny. You would have liked him," I finished.

"I bet I would have."

We sat in silence for a long time. It should have been weird or awkward. But it wasn't.

"Sorry to unload. If you have any emotional baggage you'd like to dump on me, I think it's only fair."

Michaela laughed. "Maybe that should be for a second date. You don't have to apologize. For talking. About anything. I just . . ." She paused. "I just like the sound of your voice."

"Oh. Um."

"Even if I kind of want to throw things at your family."

"Yeah. It's a reasonable response." I grinned at her in spite of myself. "If you don't want to tell me your secrets, maybe you should just do my homework for me."

"Lacey told me if I did that I'd never be allowed in the blue room again. And I need the hours for the community service requirement."

"Always fucking *Lacey*," I said. "Fine, then just check my work."

"You got it."

Love and math, Rachel.

Neither make much sense to me at all.

Sincerely,

Brynn

Folder:	Drafts
To:	Rachel@msnbc.com
From:	Brynnieh0401@gmail.com
Date:	November 27
Subject:	The kiss

Dear Rachel Maddow,

I didn't have to work today, so Michaela and I met at the library again. I told her my synopsis of *Grapes of Wrath*, which I was assigned to read over break. (It sucked and then the baby died. Fucking dust bowl.)

Afterward we wandered around downtown. There isn't much left there anymore. The department stores closed before I was born. Even so, the gazebo in the park had recently been painted, and it glistened in the damp November afternoon.

"It's pretty here, sometimes. When it's quiet," I said.

Michaela nodded, lost in thought.

"What's hiding in your brain, under all the curls?" I asked her.

She looked over at me. Then she leaned over and kissed me under the gazebo arch. I kissed her back, and the world melted into a swirl of cold and hot.

We rode separate buses home. But Michaela texted me later to see how I was doing.

"Asshole stepfather run off with the circus?"

I laughed. "Maybe. I haven't checked recently."

"I'll keep my fingers crossed."

I fell asleep, phone on top of my chest, like she was there. I dreamt of her soft skin against mine, and of kissing her under the bare trees.

Sincerely,

Brynn

Folder: Drafts
To: Rachel@msnbc.com
From: Brynnieh0401@gmail.com
Date: November 28
Subject: Runoff far, far away

Dear Rachel Maddow,

I kind of wish I actually e-mailed you what is now basically my journal. Because what's going down is exactly like the stuff you cover, only not, because it's lame high school, only yes it is, because maybe it never actually changes.

At least I got two extra days off of school for the first days of buck season. But then it was back to the blue room, and my face has this weird yellowish bruise, and yeah, my mom doesn't love me and stuff. She picked Fart Weasel over me. That was clear again and again. I realized she basically left when my dad did.

So I was less than polite to Lacey, who came over to me first thing in the morning.

"What . . . happened?" she said.

"It's a long story. Not a good one," I said.

"Okay." She sat there in silence a few moments. "Is there anything I can do?"

"No." I sighed. "Maybe help propel me to political achievement."

"That would involve talking about the superintendent selection committee seat."

I sighed.

"You're in this now, Brynn. Did you mean it? Do you really care?"

If I thought about it, if I literally focused on something outside of the nose on my face, I had to admit that I did. I have been listening to too much of you, Rachel. You and your stupid cheerful explanations of the news and shit. Damn it all.

I nodded.

"Then you'll have to keep acting like it."

I nodded again, but fortunately class started. At lunch, Lacey tried again.

"So, about getting people to vote for you . . ."

"Lacey, honest to God, why do you care about this? You could have just *done* this."

"Brynn, I do care. But my parents would kill me if they had to drive me to yet another extracurricular activity. Like I need more time in the van listening to them tell me how I could still homeschool even though I'm almost in college. And sitting in selection committee meetings sounds sooooo boring. Not that that should deter *you*." She smiled. "Besides, I asked my prof at my Saturday community college class if I could use this as my semester project. She loved the idea. If you could run for something next semester, too, you'd be doing me a real solid for the second section of the class."

I flipped her off. "Whatever. Just tell me what to do." I paused. "And I have this friend in journalism who loves this sort of thing. Justin. Good guy. He wants to help. Me. You know. With this."

Rachel, I really am so damn smooth.

Lacey smiled at me. "Yes. He said as much at the last Academic Bowl practice. I'll e-mail you both my plan. " She rolled away.

As I walked through the parking lot at the end of the day, I heard a voice call my name. Michaela caught up to me and put a hand on my shoulder. "Brynn, wait." I stopped. Her dark curls fanned nimbus-like from the wind.

"Hi," I said, feeling shy for the first time in about a decade.

"Hey." She grinned. "What's up?"

"Politics."

"Ah," she said. "Are you going home now?"

"I don't have to."

"Do you want to tell me about superintendents? Bet it's sexy. We could get something to eat. Or something." She shivered a little, her cheeks growing pinker.

"Sexy superintendent. I'll float that to Lacey as a way to win votes."

Michaela and I soon settled into a corner booth at Eat'n Park. I have a weakness for their Smiley Cookies.

"You're so cool, Brynn."

I half choked on my Smiley Cookie. "What do you mean?"

"Are you kidding? Everyone I'm in class with either worships or fears Adam. And then there's you. You do neither. You stand up to him. You have conviction and courage and . . ." She shook her head. "That's so impressive, Brynn."

"I guess." I shrugged. "I'm *still* not the best student, though."

"Sarah says you used to be," Michaela said. She looked like she immediately regretted it.

"You talked to her about me?"

"No. Not exactly. Just after that day at lunch she agreed with Adam that you had so much promise and let it all go to waste."

I rolled my eyes.

"I spilled my soda on Adam 'accidentally' after that."

"That's hot," I said. I thought for a minute. "I don't know about potential." I stalled by licking an eye off of my cookie. "I used to be better. At school."

"Everybody struggles with something."

"You don't," I said. "You could do math tied up, blindfolded, with a chicken pecking on your neck."

"What the hell are you talking about?" she said.

"I have to try really, really hard. It's not easy. It never was. But before I was happy and then everything kind of fell apart. Like, in my life. You know. Nick. Stepfather. And I didn't have enough energy to try."

"I hear that." Michaela leaned across the table. "Things kind of fell apart for me, too. At my old school. I moved here to try to . . . be different. Turn over a new leaf. So maybe I can help you with math or whatever. And you can help me."

"Turn over a new leaf? You seem pretty green already." Maybe Michaela really did have secrets.

Michaela looked at her coffee. "All your caring about making things better. It could rub off on me."

"Oooh-kay." I threw her mad side-eye. "Sure thing, peer tutor."

"I'm serious." She laughed. "You don't even know. I'll tell you some-time after I'm sure you won't stop talking to me because of it."

"That would never happen." I shook my head for emphasis.

Michaela coughed but didn't say anything.

We finished our coffee in silence.

She followed me when I got up. My side brushed up against hers when we both tried to wedge through the exit first.

"Well. I'll see you, then," I said.

"Yeah," she said. She put her face close to mine, so we were practi-cally nose-to-nose.

"Sure," I whispered. She took the inch between us until her lips met mine.

I'd only ever kissed Sarah, and now Michaela. *Really* kissed, anyway. At the end, Sarah was arid and prickly like a desert cactus. Michaela, standing here with me there, was waves and sea glass and sunshine, her lips salty and warm and perfect.

Sincerely,
Brynn

Folder:	Drafts
To:	Rachel@msnbc.com
From:	Brynnieh0401@gmail.com
Date:	December 10
Subject:	On the trail

Dear Rachel Maddow,

Team Lacey and Justin apparently had to get together several evenings last week to strategize about how to win the superintendent selection committee seat. Since this was a special runoff, there was no official "start" to our campaign. But Lacey needed something for her college class, so she'd convinced me to get on it.

"So you talked about me," I asked Lacey.

"Well, not just you. Academic Bowl season is just around the corner."

"Uh-huh."

"He's really funny."

"Yes."

"I like freckles."

"Are you a thing? You and Justin?" I said.

Lacey blushed. "I believe we are. He's great."

"Yes, he's lovely. For a guy." I snickered. I decided not to harass Lacey about her man friend, lest she decide to grill me about Michaela in retaliation. "So what did yinz all come up with for me? Does assassination come into play at all?"

"No, sadly we can't kill Adam. Instead, we were thinking you should go after the jocks."

"Go after the whoseit what now?"

"Adam's a big-deal wrestler. We all know that. But that doesn't make him a 'jock's jock,' as Justin says."

"You lost me at 'we can't kill Adam,' I'm afraid," I said.

"You need to go out to the people and give them what they want. And what they want is someone like them. Justin and I feel you are more like most of the students here. More than Adam. And we think you can appeal to the voters' needs and wants."

"Actually, can we talk more about *you* and Justin here for a second. . . ."

"Brynn, Michaela volunteered to help you."

"Say no more," I said, putting up my hands.

Thus it came to be that Michaela, Bianca, Lance, Greg, Riley, and I took shifts at a table outside of the cafeteria with life-sized Steelers cut-outs. I thought about getting a Tom Brady in your honor, Rachel, but I just couldn't bring myself to do it. That'd cause a coup in Steeler country for sure. Lance's dad donated a pair of tickets to raffle off. Bless the blue room season-ticket-holder families. Michaela handed out "Brynn for the Win" stickers to kids who entered the raffle. A freshman rando won them. But that freshman rando *voter* said he hoped I got to select the next school superintendent.

Look at me, Rachel! I'm part of democracy in action!

Or maybe I'm just a political cog grinding slowly in the campaign machine.

But you have to start somewhere.

Sincerely,
Brynn

Folder:	Drafts
To:	Rachel@msnbc.com
From:	Brynnieh0401@gmail.com
Date:	December 14
Subject:	First lady

Dear Rachel Maddow,

Today I went with Michaela to her friend Jen's house. Jen is a senior Michaela met through peer tutoring. Lacey thought going to a party was a good Idea to try to raise my public profile. She would not have been happy to learn that I mostly just hid in a corner with my lady friend.

"So, let me get this straight," said Michaela. "Adam made T-shirts for every single Westing High student?"

"All two hundred and fifty-three of them—you got it," I said.

"How come I didn't get one? They sound great."

Adam had upped my Steelers bid by making a Penguins-Pirates mash-up T-shirt that was pretty epic. I admit I was annoyed I couldn't have one because I would have been campaigning against myself.

"Yeah," I said. "Adam has his own super PAC in his dad. Remind me to ask the new superintendent candidates about their campaign finance views if I get this stupid committee seat."

"When." Michaela smiled, pulling me close. "When you get it."

"We'll see," I said, but Michaela muffled my words. Her mouth indicated she was clearly done talking about politics for the evening.

I might have raised my profile a little with one person at that party. But really she was the one who mattered most to me. I could tell Lacey that I came to the party to try to be social and meet the voters. It wouldn't exactly be a lie. I had met and been very social with one voter.

It's the best new thing in the world, Rachel.

Sincerely,

Brynn

Folder: Drafts
To: Rachel@msnbc.com
From: Brynnieh0401@gmail.com
Date: December 17
Subject: Political briefs

Dear Rachel Maddow,

So here's a thing: If underwear is returned to Aerie, even if the person swears up and down that it's never been worn, then out it goes. If it is found in the changing room and bears evidence that it has been tried on, out it goes. Last week this one shipment came in with defects and we gave it a mad discount, but no one wanted undies with obviously faulty stitching.

Anyway, the point here is that there was a lot of extra underwear that had nowhere to go. Technically it was to be "destroyed," but I decided to borrow it in the name truth and justice. After Adam's T-shirt stunt, I had to seriously up my game to capture the people's hearts and minds and butts before the superintendent committee seat runoff. I only had a week to make up ground. Erin said no to my plan about a thousand times when I asked her for all of it, but she eventually gave in to say that if it went missing, she'd conduct a search and ask questions until it showed up again.

Thank you, Citizen Erin.

Thus I came to get a ride from Leigh way too early this morning, since I had many assloads of boybriefs and cheekies to bring to Westing High. He parked down the street and helped me carry my sketchy garbage bags up to the school. There was a small problem that every door we tried was locked. But then Space God, perhaps because of some sort of clerical error, decided to deliver unto Brynn once more. Mr. Bill, the sixty-year-old hottie of janitorial services, came out a side exit while Leigh and I were staring at it.

"Uh, hi, Mr. Bill," I said.

"Hiding bodies?" he said, eyeing the bags.

"Actually, I'm trying to enact a peaceful yet poignant protest against this guy Adam, who is the devil's own testicles." (Those were Lacey's words for what we were doing, minus the testicle bit.)

Mr. Bill raised an eyebrow at the bags. "Yeah, okay," he said. He held the door open for us and looked up into the doorframe. "The cameras aren't turned on, by the way. I don't boot up the system until the first bell. They are a pain in the ol' keister, you know?"

"Mr. Bill, I hear you," I said. "Thank you."

Leigh nodded to him, and Mr. Bill nodded back.

"Good luck. Your brother was a good kid," he said, and he let the door shut behind me and Leigh.

Nick had believed in being kind to people like Mr. Bill. "Everyone is important, Brynnie," Nick used to say to me. " 'Cause you never know who could get you your next fix. Or pull your sorry drunk ass out of a ditch. It could be any bitch or junkie, you know?"

Again, my real-life examples aren't the greatest, but you get what I'm saying? This was Nick's lifestyle. An addict with a heart of gold, who was right that a person should be nice to everyone. Score one for Nick, patron saint of his ridiculous sister.

"You don't have to do this," I told Leigh. "Don't you have to get to work?"

"Eventually," he said. "But I haven't pulled a prank in years. This used to be my *life*. I was king of this kind of stuff. And it annoys Erin to know I'm helping. That's a hobby of mine." He winked at me. "Let's do this."

With that, we were off. We decked the halls with boughs of undies, fa la la la la, la, la, la, la. We only had enough for the first floor, though Leigh made a lovely arch over the doorway out of duct tape and thongs. I pulled out my a stack of construction paper "Strip Off the Spin, Vote for Brynn" signs and Scotch tape, generously crafted by the red and yellow roomers who worshipped Bianca. We rainbowed the lockers and the doors. It was like an Aerie-sponsored Pride event. Up and down the hall, the letters on the signs spelled out "It's Not a Sin, Vote for Brynn." Lacey thought it was essential to rhyme to "make an impact on the voters."

Leigh and I were finished before 6:00 a.m. He took me to a diner nearby. I scarfed pancakes and coffee. Leigh watched me.

"He'd have been proud of you," he said. "Real proud."

I stopped chewing. The pancakes in my mouth sat there like a wad of wet paper.

"Too bad he's not here to see," I said, barely swallowing.

"Yeah." We didn't say anything after that. Leigh dropped me off right at the front of the school, in full view of everyone. I walked up the sidewalk, trying to look innocent. I got into the school, and the underwear was gloriously still up.

"Well, hello, Ms. Harper." Mr. Maynard greeted me by the steps, almost as if he were waiting for me.

"Well, hello," I said. "Wow, would you look at this? This is for me?" I tried to feign surprise.

"So it would seem," he said wryly. "You wouldn't happen to know anything about this, would you?"

"No, sir. I kind of like it, though." I grinned, looking around. "Girl power!"

"Yes. Well, Mr. Bill apparently was occupied on the third floor with a plumbing issue, and has no idea how someone would have gotten in to do it. I spoke with your junior cohort"—he paused—"but I don't think they would have done it, either."

Nope. *Certainly* those fine, upstanding Applied folks had no part in this.

"But this should come down. It's causing quite a stir."

I looked around. The hormone level from the presence of all the fancy underwear was palpable. "Well, it has my name on it. And it's not right that Mr. Bill should have to clean something like this up all by himself," I added.

Mr. Maynard looked like he was fighting a smile.

"Let me run downstairs and ask Mr. Grimm if I can have a few minutes to help clean this up," I said.

Mr. Maynard nodded. I took the steps two at a time to the blue room. I burst in, and the whole room cheered.

"Brilliant!" said Bianca.

"You go, girl," said Lacey.

"I don't know what any of you are talking about," said Mr. Grimm, handing me the trash bags I had stashed under his desk. "You'll be needing these."

I nodded and went upstairs to unhook the rogue freedom undies from the hall. I placed them carefully into the bags and stashed them in the blue room until Leigh picked me up after school. If only Nick could have seen it. My stomach hurt thinking of him. It was an epic prank that would have brought him so much joy. What's the point of a victory, even a small one, if you can't share it with the person with whom you most want?

I guess I'll share it with Michaela. She isn't a replacement for Nick. Or Sarah, even. But she's pretty magnificent all on her own.

And I'll share it with you, Rachel. You're at least back from vacation. So I'll see you soon.

Sincerely,

Brynn

Folder: Drafts
To: Rachel@msnbc.com
From: Brynnieh0401@gmail.com
Date: December 18
Subject: Two days

Dear Rachel Maddow,

In two days the people will decide between Adam and me. Justin says that while I am trailing, the underwear scored me a lot of points. This gives me a little hope for the future of the world.

But only a little.

Speaking of underwear, Lacey-love had energized Justin so much he found me everywhere he could to give me extra moral support. Including at freaking Aerie.

"Brynn, I'm told your grades are way up and you can come back to the paper."

"My grades are not 'way up.' And know that I will be having a conversation with a certain mutual acquaintance of ours that my academic progress ought to be confidential. Oh my God, Justin, you couldn't have talked to me at school?"

"Oh, come on. She does it out of love. And you need a two-point-three, dude! Two-point-three! That's sad."

I gaped at him. Boybriefs and undies withered around him, caught in the cross fire.

"Okay, sorry. Dick move. Sorry, sorry."

"Things suck at home, you know," I said.

"I didn't."

"And don't even get me started on . . . you know what? You *are* a dick."

"Yes. Totally. One hundred percent. I'm sorry," he said.

"Fine. Go away. I'm working. And if you ask me to pick something out for your girlfriend, I will choke you."

Justin's islands of freckles melded to form a continent at the word "girlfriend."

"I am just saying, Brynn," he said, clearing his throat, "that maybe you won't win this thing. But the paper is there. We could use you. You could help me find out whether Adam really was involved with setting the War Memorial fire. Expose town corruption. That kind of thing."

"Go away," I said.

He did. Honestly, someone should tell him print is dead. That no one reads that anyway. That it doesn't matter.

I'd have told him. But I didn't have the urge to argue things I didn't believe to be true.

Sincerely,

Brynn

Folder:	Drafts
To:	Rachel@msnbc.com
From:	Brynnieh0401@gmail.com
Date:	December 21
Subject:	Super Tuesday Revisited

Dear Rachel Maddow,

This morning was a hymn to Space God.

Michaela waited outside the main entrance for me, even though the wind chill was in the single digits. "Hey there, Underwear Queen."

"That's a terrible nickname," I said, kissing the one uncovered square inch of her face.

"High Priestess of Thongs."

"Please no," I said.

"Bralette Viceroy?"

"Stop. Now you're just making shit up."

"Am not. Viceroys are like governors who work for kings. They are also a type of butterfly."

"It is too early and too cold for this discussion."

"Fine." She held the door open for me, and I followed her into the lobby.

"You nervous? Runoff is today."

"Yeah. Kind of."

"You did a good thing, Brynn. Even if you don't get to help pick a school superintendent. I'm proud of you."

"Wow," I said. "You know, I don't remember the last time anyone has said that to me."

Michaela peeled off her scarf. "I'll put a note in my phone so I remember to tell you every week. Because it's true."

Sarah had never once said she was proud of me. Probably because she had never once *felt* pride in anything I did.

"Though, in addition, I also realized you could probably buy me sexy underwear at a discount."

At least I could still blame the raw December wind for the fact that my face reddened darker than a tomato. "Um. Would you *like* me to buy you sexy underwear?"

"Well, I could buy it. But you could save me money."

"Forty percent." I tried to swallow, but damn that Pennsylvania winter for also drying out my mouth entirely. "Sometimes I can get extra on clearance."

"There you go. More matching sets for me!" Michaela leaned in until her breath tickled my ear. "I'd be happy to share with you."

"We aren't the same size," I said. Michaela was tall and stick thin. I had the body type of a tater tot.

"That isn't what I meant."

I couldn't think of anything to say. Fucking cold froze my brain, too. I just stared at her until she laughed.

"Speechless. Well. That doesn't happen often. I'm going to take that as a compliment."

"I'm working most of winter break."

"Noted," she said.

The first bell rang, and I realized people streamed around us.

"You are glorious in your perfection," I blurted.

Now Michaela's face took on a berrylike tone. "Good luck today, Brynn."

"Thanks."

My legs fortunately cooperated in moving me away from Michaela, toward the cafeteria. The runoff started as soon as the school doors opened, and the person chosen to help select the next superintendent would be announced at the end of the day. A table was already set up, with ballot boxes in place. I was unsurprised and pissed to see familiar faces manning the polls.

"What are you doing?" I asked Sarah.

"We *are* Student Government," Adam answered for her. "We run these kind of things."

"That doesn't seem fair," I said.

"Adam and Sarah aren't doing anything with the runoff, Brynn," Nancy said as she walked up behind the table and slid out a folding chair. "I am. And I'll keep it fair."

I trusted her more than Adam, and probably Sarah if I was being honest. Even if rumor had it Nancy and Sarah were together now, Nancy had always been good people the few times we'd hung out.

"Okay." I nodded at her. I turned to Adam. "You shouldn't be within fifty feet," I said.

"I'm not trying to convince people to vote for me," he said.

The second bell rang. I had missed homeroom completely, but Mr. Grimm probably figured it was runoff-related.

"Then why are you here?"

People rushed out of their classrooms and hurried to their first-period classes.

A few kids I knew from the auto shop next to the journalism lab looked at the table. "Oh, is this the thing we're supposed to vote for today. The underwear thing?"

I opened my mouth, but Adam beat me. "No. That happened already. This is for something else."

"What? No, it's not. This is for the superintendent selection committee!" I said.

The kid looked from me to Adam. "Uh. Yeah. That. Will it take long? If I'm late again, I'm going to get detention."

"Only about ten minutes," Adam jumped in. "You can get started by presenting your student ID."

"No, you don't. It'll take two seconds!" I said. I glared at Sarah. At Nancy. Neither of them spoke.

"Whatever, man. I gotta go." And the kid walked off.

"Wait," I called after him, but I lost him in a sea of bodies and backpacks.

"*This* is your game? Are you fucking kidding me?" I said.

"It might take you a while to read the ballot," Adam said.

"He isn't stupid!" I yelled.

"And everyone *does* need their ID. All student elections require proof of attendance to vote. It's in the school's bylaws."

"Put there by you, no doubt, without anybody noticing," I said. I looked at Sarah. "Does he have some dirt on you or something? Why are you putting up with this?" She wouldn't look me in the eye.

"It might have been one of my better ideas last year," said Adam.

"No one brings their ID to school."

Adam shrugged. "Pretty sure everyone I know does." Adam glanced at Nancy and then at Sarah. "See you later."

I was so pissed I couldn't even look at either of them. Crazy thoughts bounced around in my head. Maybe I should convince Justin to go to the principal with the rumors about Adam being involved in the War Memorial fire, even if we didn't technically have any proof.

I marched to Mr. Maynard's office without a definite plan.

"Sorry, dear, he's out until this afternoon," said Esther.

I swore under my breath all the way to the blue room.

"There you are," said Mr. Grimm. "Has the runoff started?"

"Adam and his team have started a campaign of voter suppression! And you have to have your stupid Westing High ID to even get a ballot. Did you know that?"

Mr. Grimm frowned. "I did not."

I slid into my desk. "Is there anything I can do? You don't even need your ID to get books out of the library. Who is going to lie to vote in a stupid runoff?" I asked him. "Like, two hundred people go to this school. You're telling me Nancy or whoever is manning the table won't know if someone doesn't go here?"

"I'm sorry, Brynn, I don't know. I don't usually run those sorts of things. I'll see what I can find out."

When Mr. Maynard got into school, he and Mr. Grimm looked up the student activity bylaws. Turns out that the ID thing was real. It conveniently went into effect in September. Mr. Maynard had signed off on them without really paying attention. Because why should he?

Of course Adam changed the ID rule. Of course he wanted fewer people to vote. Of course he targeted the people more likely to vote for *me*.

Because that is the one sure way guys like Adam get to keep power.

Sincerely,

Brynn

Folder: Drafts
To: Rachel@msnbc.com
From: Brynnieh0401@gmail.com
Date: December 21
Subject: Further Election Coverage

Dear Rachel Maddow,

Adam won. Turnout was incredibly low. I got 30 percent of the vote.

"That's more than you thought you'd get," said Lacey after it was announced.

"Yeah," I said.

"You thought you'd get five people," she said. "He did not win by a landslide, which is what I *know* you are thinking. That was really close."

"Yeah."

"And not to kick you when you're down, but you didn't actually *want* to help select a new superintendent."

"Yeah, I know." I sighed.

But I had started to want it, fuck me. In theory.

"It's just the point of the thing. Adam won. Guys like Adam *always* win. He can put this on his application to Harvard or whatever," I said.

"Actually, I heard he wants to go to Princeton," said Bianca.

I glared at her.

"Sorry." She shrugged.

Lacey patted my leg sympathetically. She had been optimistic, as word in the hall was that everyone knew that Adam was an awful tool demon taint. But he was a handsome, popular, *wealthy* tool demon taint. Holy fucking pundits.

I slumped in my chair, not paying much attention or doing anything. What was there to do?

"Lacey?" I asked later.

"Yes?"

"Where do you think you'll go? To college, I mean."

"Well . . ." she said.

"It's an Ivy, isn't it?

"Yes," she said, without her board.

"Where?"

"Penn."

"Like, Penn State?"

"No, the University of Pennsylvania. My grandparents and parents both went there, and Grandma and Grandpa still live in Philly. Mom and Dad work remotely, so we are going to move there. I have specialists there, and Justin's first choice is Penn or Drexel next year. I applied early decision, so I could know soon." Her face lit up. "I'm not going to lie. I'm pretty confident I'll get in."

"Well," I said. "That's the best new thing in the world, Lace."

And it is, Rachel. Even if it means I'll have to somehow survive life at Westing with Adam and without her.

Sincerely,

Brynn

Folder: Drafts
To: Rachel@msnbc.com
From: Brynnieh0401@gmail.com
Date: December 22
Subject: The Last Word (about the election)

Dear Rachel Maddow,

I have been hanging out with Leigh and Erin a lot lately, and I have formed a new life plan. I'm going to sell a lot of underwear, because this is where I see my future going. After I turn eighteen, I can move out. Without the threat of Mom or Fart Weasel, I could even quit school. Leigh got a new gig at a sporting goods store, so he could get me a position there. Then I could work with Leigh *and* Erin.

I briefly reconsidered dropping out when I got my grades. There were mostly all Bs, which let me tell you, was a freaking miracle. I also got an A in civics! This put Brynnie's cumulative score to 2.0 even. Hot damn. This made me eligible for sports and sewing club and Student Government! I could now make school-sanctioned voodoo puppets of Adam and stick them with pins at the public forums.

It brings me a small measure of satisfaction that you need a 2.3 (and thus better grades) to be on the paper than you do to be on Student Government.

The paper. I cringed a little at that one. I was so close.

The paper and Lacey and Mr. Grimm are the three reasons that give me pause in my new life plan. Mr. Grimm actually stopped me from leaving the blue room after my crushing defeat to Adam.

"Stay with me for a moment," he said.

"I have to get to work."

"This will be quick."

"Um. Okay."

"Do you still write your letters? The ones you *don't* turn in to me?"

"What do you mean?"

"You are always muttering to your laptop. Are you writing to Rachel?"

Oh, so he's on a first name basis with you, too, Rachel?

"Maybe. Sometimes," I said.

"Brynn, you are a lovely writer. Eloquent, even poetic, in your way. You are so, so smart. Your life doesn't have to follow . . ." He stopped and considered. "Any path. Your path isn't determined yet. You can do anything."

"I'm not going early decision to the University of Pennsylvania," I said.

"Well, maybe not, because that's not what you want. But you have more passion and drive than most people. I'd hate to see that all go to waste. In case no one else has ever told you this, Brynn, I believe in you. I think you could do great things. What inspires you, Brynn? Do the world a favor. Find that thing and pursue it. And don't let the bastards get you down." He clapped me on the shoulder. "There is no glory in one path over another. There is no shame in work that doesn't require a college degree. I just want you to know you have options. You shouldn't give up a dream because other people make you feel like you aren't worth investing in yourself."

Well, hot damn, Mr. Grimm, getting all deep and shit.

That night as I neatly clipped bralettes onto hangers, I thought about what he said. What *did* I care about? I didn't want Adam and his demon posse running the world unchecked, but that ship seems to have sailed. When I really thought about it, I realized amidst the bras that I was so terribly cliché as to want fucking love. My chest still twinged a little when I thought about Sarah, but it full-on felt ready to explode when I thought about Michaela. And if I'm being 100 percent, ultra fuckballs honest, the thing I loved most was the stupid school paper.

But Michaela didn't have a strict GPA requirement.

There's that.

Sincerely,

Brynn

Folder:	Drafts
To:	Rachel@msnbc.com
From:	Brynnieh0401@gmail.com
Date:	December 24
Subject:	Happy Holidays

Dear Rachel Maddow,

You're on a break. Merry Christmas.

Mom and Fart Weasel informed me that I would attend Christmas Eve services with them. I think it worried them both that I didn't even try to argue. One, I knew it was pointless. Two, I kind of liked it. They always darkened the sanctuary and passed out candles to hold while we sing "Silent Night." The choir entrance, the songs, the baby Jesus laid in a manger, the long-ass sermon, all of it is done in near night. But at last they light the candles and sing *in heavenly peace*. Then all the lights come up, and we belt out "Joy to the World." One of my first memories of Nick was at Christmas Eve church. He got so excited during "Joy to the World" that he started to shake, his entire body lit up like the tree and wreaths around us.

Now Nick's light is snuffed out like a candle after the final hymn. Even his memory is dim, faded by the drug use that ended him. Nick *was* Christmas. Now Christmas just means another year with him gone.

Afterward we got pizza. We always open presents on Christmas Eve. Since I have a job, I got Fart Weasel new socks. I got Mom a box of candy and a book of inspirational quotes. She loves that shit.

"Socks," said Fart Weasel.

"Thanks, Brynn," said Mom.

They got me a dictionary. A *used* dictionary, from the looks of the sticker on the back.

"To help you at school," Mom said. I thought she looked a little guilty. Maybe I just hoped she did. I don't think either of them expected me to get them anything, especially not something they might actually want.

Technically I got Fart Weasel socks to troll both him *and* Mom, but neither seemed to have picked up on that. Just as well.

"Thanks," I said.

We sat in awkward silence for a full minute.

"Well, tired. Night." I went to my room.

I lay on my bed and looked at my dictionary. The words tumbled around on the page like usual. I reached up and shoved it onto my shelf, next to the dusty candle they'd given me last year.

I hope you had a great holiday, Rachel.

I hope you catch a lot of ice fish, or whatever it is you do with this vacation.

Sincerely,

Brynn

Folder:	Inbox
To:	Brynnieh0401@gmail.com
From:	ChemicaLacey@gmail.com
Date:	December 27
Subject:	Brave

Dear Brynn,

I want you to know that even though the epistolary format is better for expressing myself, it is still a giant pain in my cushioned butt. So you better appreciate this.

Oh, I mean, Merry Christmas!

I really admire what you did last semester, Brynn. You saw a need and took action. Not enough people do that these days. And you kept with it even though you weren't sure you really wanted to. Again, that is so brave. People call me "brave" all the time, and it annoys me. As if my mere existence is some sort of war. It's not. I don't think I'm any braver than another person just trying to live life. I just can't do stairs.

Anyway, my point is that I think things must be tough at home, even though you don't talk about it much. I'm glad I got to be your resident peer tutor, and your friend.

Love,
Lacey

P.S. I got an A in my gov class at the community college. I have the 201 version next term. My teacher doesn't believe that you get away with swearing that much at school. I said if she met Mr. Grimm, she'd understand.

Folder:	Drafts
To:	Rachel@msnbc.com
From:	Brynnieh0401@gmail.com
Date:	January 1
Subject:	Drift away

Dear Rachel Maddow,

I have sold and exchanged and returned and stocked and sold more under-wear in the last week than anyone rightfully should. I worked every second I could, spent as much time with Michaela as I could, and stayed at home long enough to fulfill my Cinderella duties and sleep. Mom and Fart Weasel haven't been exactly nice since the candy and the socks, but they haven't tried to keep me from going out, either.

Michaela met me outside of the store on New Year's Eve. We closed at six o'clock, which was good, because I was ready to stick boyshorts down the throat of the next person who asked me if we had a size extra-extra-small.

Westing had a bunch of New Year's Eve stuff that was mostly for kids. Michaela and I watched a puppet show and a recorder demonstration.

"Do you play an instrument?" I asked her as we examined an illuminated ice sculpture of a piano.

"Nope. You?"

"Nope," I said. "But I am a gifted mime."

"Really?" she said.

"No."

"Oh. Bummer." She laughed.

"What do your parents do?" I asked. It occurred to me that Michaela never really talked about them.

"My mom's a lawyer. My dad does business stuff."

"Here in Westing?"

"No. They are still in Michigan. I live here with my grandma."

I thought about that. We moved on to a horse sculpture.

"Why?" I asked.

Michaela sighed. "It's a long story."

"I have time," I said.

"Brynn . . ." she started. "I wasn't so great at my last school. Like, I was a good student. But I did some stupid stuff. I needed to clear my head. So my parents sent me here. For a fresh start. And I wasn't even going to . . . I mean, I was just going to focus . . . but then you were . . ."

I threw her a blank look.

"I just would rather not talk about it. It's seriously not worth it. It's nothing against you. And my grandma is old and doesn't remember, so that's why I don't have you over."

I knew that there was no way I'd have Michaela over to my house, so that part I got. But Sarah had been like me. She narrated every thought that went through her head, every moment of her day. Maybe not knowing much about Michaela would be refreshing.

Or maybe it would feel really fucking weird.

"Okay," I said.

"Really?" she said.

I shrugged. "Whatever happened doesn't seem to have affected your math skills."

Michaela grinned. "Good to know you like me for my brain."

That was true. I liked every part of her. I tried to communicate that as clearly as possible in the empty theater where we enjoyed avant-garde animation.

At least, I think that was what was playing. We weren't really paying attention to the screen.

I kissed her good night at 12:05 under the fireworks. The buses ran late for the holiday. She boarded hers and then I mine, and we texted swoony emojis to each other until my battery died.

I decided it didn't matter what Michaela didn't want to tell me. Maybe she'd spill it all when she was ready. What mattered is that when most people made me want to run and hide in bed forever, Michaela made me want to stay awake. Also in bed, if I'm being totally honest, but out in the world, too.

Though, it *was* still a world in which Adam won, and I lost. Because that's what I did. Lose. It was my one consistent, defining skill.

Adam's was winning.

The covers twisted tighter around my legs as I turned over and over trying to get comfortable.

I eventually dozed off, tangled and alone.

Happy New Year, Rachel. I'll be back to school tomorrow, and you'll be back on the air. Who knows what the new year will bring us both.

Sincerely,

Brynn

Folder:	Sent
To:	Brynnieh0401@gmail.com
From:	Egrimm@westing.pa.edu
Date:	January 3
Subject:	RE: Sorry this is late

Dear Rachel Maddow,

[Mr. Grimm, I know you told me to dictate this like I usually do. So I am. Rachel and I have reached a deep level of honesty, though. Not that anything probably shocks you after years teaching the Applied classes.]

I marched into school today in a decent mood. Even if I dreaded the thought of seeing Adam, Michaela had texted me all Tuesday and Wednesday. I think maybe she felt like she needed to make up for the "spooky secrets she doesn't want to share" thing. I also cheered myself up with the vague notion that in less than two months, I'd turn eighteen and would be a legal adult who could do with my life whatever I saw fit. An invisible countdown clock ticked happily down in my head, when a hand emerged from a set of lockers and yanked me over.

"Yo, what?" I yelled, trying to maintain my balance. "What the hell?"

Justin glanced around furtively, the owner of the mysterious grabby hand.

"Shhh," he said. "Please don't scream. We need to talk."

"Listen, Justin, I don't know what the hell you are doing, but you could have just found me in the blue room. . . ."

"I know, I know. But there would be too many witnesses down there. Please. Just come with me. You won't be harmed."

If that isn't the most compelling reason *not* to follow someone, I don't know what is. [Brynn, the creative nonfiction assignment you were to make up was "Why losing isn't the end of the world." Did you forget the *nonfiction* aspect of this?] But Justin dragged me down a corridor to another set of stairs. I could have fought back, but part of me was curious to see what this was about. The other part knew where we were headed.

"You can let go. I'll go to the journalism lair willingly," I told him.

Justin let go. He pushed open the double doors, and I followed him into my former happy place. Six or seven other newspaper kids appeared to be waiting for me. One of them was Sarah. I stopped, took one look at her, and spun on my heel to get the hell out of Dodge. I ran straight into Justin.

"How did you do that?" I asked him.

He grinned.

I sighed and turned around. "Fine," I said. "What?" I asked Sarah.

"Listen. I know this is weird. But we need your help," Sarah said.

"You need *my* help?" I laughed out loud. "You can't be serious."

"Oh, we are," she said.

"I'm leaving. For good. I'm so over and done with all of this," I said, and looked at her directly in the eye. "And I thought you quit the paper. You know what? I don't even care."

"I came back for this semester," Sarah said. Her eyes dropped to the floor. "Hear us out. You know, we have a common enemy. And in trying circumstances, that is a compelling enough reason to come together once more."

"What?"

"There was kind of a shake-up in Student Government over break. Adam said some things that weren't cool. I wasn't a big fan of his voter-suppression tactics. None of us knew about the whole ID requirement. I'm done with him," she said.

"Oh, now you're done with him," I said. "What, did someone finally get something linking him to the War Memorial fire? Is that what it takes? Major crime?"

Sarah frowned deeply, her forehead creasing. I knew that was a sign I'd said something that really bothered her.

"You know he was coeditor of the news section," she said, ignoring my comment. "But he quit right before the superintendent runoff. Said he had to focus on 'finishing strong' in the spring. And he wants to focus on winning student body president next year. That's the most important thing to him, Brynn. Student body president."

The other paper people nodded in agreement.

"Good for him. This doesn't have anything to do with me," I said.

Though, the idea of Adam-in-charge-of-even-stupid-shit did still make my skin crawl.

"I know," said Sarah. "But we also have reason to believe he is going to try to take down the school paper." [BRYNN, I AM NOT YOUR PEER HERE. I HOPE THIS STORY IS GOING SOMEWHERE GOOD. You know, it occurs to me that you turned this in. So, you didn't drop out even though I've overheard you fantasize about it. I'll just read this to the end and then come back and make comments. That will likely be more useful for us both.]

"*What?*" My voice rose to a comic octave. "The paper? That's the dumbest thing ever. Why?"

"There was that rumor that Adam might have been responsible for the War Memorial fire," said Justin. "Adam's friend Anderson claimed he was there and had pictures, but nothing ever came of that. And since *someone* refused to help me"—Justin shot me a pointed look—"I decided to look for evidence on my own," he said. "I got substantiated info from the fire chief that the *Tribune Republican* didn't publish. Someone definitely set off fireworks that caught the grass and stuff on fire. That's what turned into the five-alarm blaze. They actually found the fireworks."

Justin always slipped into newspaper prose when he talked about a juicy tip.

"Yeah, so we knew all that," I said. "Why haven't you run anything, then?"

"We can't," said Justin. "That's just it. An anonymous donor made a very generous gift to the journalism and computer labs, and we got all this." Justin swept his hand around the room. There were huge new monitors all around, and a massive printer that was churning out something as we spoke. There was a SMART Board and a flat-screen in the corner.

"Whoever gave the money said we have to stick to school-only news. No community stuff. Now Mr. McCloud said we can't run it. Maynard was forced to invoke his right to read the paper before we publish. Even the online edition! I kept trying to tell you things were getting weird down here. But you wouldn't listen!" 3-D art emerged on Justin's face. " *'Our liberty cannot be guarded but by the freedom of the press, nor that be limited without danger of losing it.'* Thomas Jefferson said that, Brynn." [Well done, Mr. Mitchell.]

Thomas Fucking Jefferson. You know who else quotes him, Rachel? You do. In *Drift*. Goddamnit motherfucker, that hit me where it hurt. Bet Sarah was behind that shit.

"Okay, okay, I get it. Adam wants to take down the free press," I said. Even as I said it, a vein or nerve or alien baby egg started to throb in my forehead.

"We think it might have been his dad. . . ."

"Oh whatever, it's basically Adam. What now? What do you want from me?"

The alien baby wiggled behind my eyes. Though, I hate to admit this, Rachel, a tiny section in the back of my brain thrilled that Sarah thought me worthy of this attempt.

"We want to hit Adam where it hurts," said Sarah.

"Where it matters. And keep him from ruining everything and save the paper. Two birds, one stone, and all that," said Justin.

"How?" I said.

"We want you to run for student body president," said Justin.

"No. Noooooo. No way in hell. You run," I said to Sarah. "This is your thing, too."

"I'm already running for vice president. You can do this. That underwear thing was inspired. We have some ideas but need help enacting them. We just need to stop Adam. We'll help you," she said.

"Who is this we?" I asked.

Justin stepped forward.

"That would be me," he said. "Obviously. And I know some people in a certain subterranean portion of the school who love you and will certainly help."

"And me," said Sarah.

Part in brain. Tiny thrill. Also activated part of brain that causes nausea. And the tiny alien baby egg.

"I hold it that a little rebellion now and then is a good thing, and as necessary in the political world as storms in the physical," said Justin. [Brynn, I have found his original source for this quote. I will give it to you and have you write a brief response to it for extra credit.]

I looked at Justin, and at Sarah and back at Justin, knowing that if I went through with this, Lacey was going to think I'd lost my mind for good. Though, she would have a project for this community college semester. A student body president election would get her a fucking A-plus-plus.

Adam had beaten me last semester using his slime mold ball sack tactics. He might have taken out my War Memorial beat, important since it encompasses the bulk of my early reporting. But now he was attacking the free press. Stupid Adam messing with *my free fucking press*.

Mark my words, Rachel. I hate Westing High. But you've made me such a damn fan of telling stories and free speech and all that shit. If I can help try to protect it in my little shithole corner of the world, then I figure I owe it to you.

And there is still the business of furthering the cause of women in politics and all. Look at what happens to the women who try to take on the dude bros. They get pushed down again and again and again.

Nevertheless, they persist.

I guess that means I fucking have to, too.

The countdown clock to my academic departure has stopped.

For now. [I am glad this had a good ending! Please see me about extra credit. You are one report card away from being allowed back on the paper.]

Sincerely,
Brynn

[Note: The original source of Mr. Mitchell's last quote is a letter from Thomas Jefferson to James Madison in 1787. Now, even that passage Mr. Mitchell cites has its problematic elements. Look it up and see what I mean. Feel free to write an extra-credit essay on that. No political figure deserves to be revered unchecked, you may agree.]

Folder: Drafts
To: Rachel@msnbc.com
From: Brynnieh0401@gmail.com
Date: January 7
Subject: . . . In love and War

Dear Rachel Maddow,

Lacey was out sick for the rest of the week, so I couldn't convince her she ought to strangle me (and Justin) for considering this. I thought Michaela would think what few marbles remained had rolled away, but she didn't seem surprised.

"You gotta do you, Brynn."

"Do you think I'm crazy?" I said.

"No. I would like someone to get Adam. He's an ass who plays dirty to get what he wants. And you might be the only woman for the job. Civic engagement looks good on you."

I grinned.

"At least this will keep you from your fantasies of dropping out. Speaking of which, you have to maintain your GPA for SGA participation. So you have to keep doing your work." She nodded at the notebook in front of me. In theory she was supposed to be helping me that very second. Maybe she was.

When Lacey returned to school, she was delighted.

"Thank God," she said. "I thought I was going to have to go to my mom's Rotary meetings. Dad offered the Masons, but I spend enough time with them as it is. I have to be here anyway! This works out well for me."

I rolled my eyes. "Glad to be of service," I said.

"You should know, though, Adam will go after you. He will go after you, and it won't be pretty. Even if you aren't running. Because he hates you."

"Tell me what you really think, Lace," I said. "This is how it has to be. No one will go against him, and then Adam will suck the rest of the soul from the building. It will be a stinking pile of devil turd."

Lacey started laughing and didn't stop for a full two minutes.

"Turd." She laughed and laughed. "Where do you get this stuff?" Lacey shook her head at me.

"I have a very active imagination," I said. "I'm sure I'll make for an interesting chapter in that memoir you'll get paid to write at that big, fancy college you're going to."

"True," she said. "Let's get to work."

Sincerely,
Brynn

Folder: Drafts
To: Rachel@msnbc.com
From: Brynnieh0401@gmail.com
Date: January 8
Subject: Going rogue

Dear Rachel Maddow,

On March 19, exactly ten weeks from today, there will be an SGA election. Before that, I have to collect enough signatures to get on the ballot. Then each candidate gets to make a commercial to be broadcast to every homeroom. Then we have a debate, campaign for a few weeks, and then we vote. So far, it's just Adam vying for student body president.

(Of fucking *course*.)

Lacey wasn't hopeful that anyone else was going to go for it, because of Adam. But because of Justin's apparent undying appreciation of the Academic Bowl captain, he was running for treasurer. I think he might be jealous of the fact that I am now the subject of a second semester project.

And since Space God is known for an extraordinary sense of humor, the Cosmic Joker put Adam directly in my path today. I'd avoided him for ages. Maybe God is into S&M, I don't know.

I do know that both Adam and I were surprised when I was walking down the hall thinking of how to get signatures for my "intent to run for SGA" petition just as Adam was exiting the boys' room and we came face-to-face.

"Oh," he said.

When placed into these sorts of situations, really, I should walk away. No, run as fast as my shapely ass can move in a pair of boybriefs. But do I do the wise thing?

"You are such a dick and I hate you," I said.

"Wow," he said, a slow smile spreading across his face. "Are you still pissed about the committee thing? Aww. Poor Brynn."

"Nope. If you are even half as smart as you think you are, you'd realize that."

The smile faded a little. "Then why are you saying such nice things? Are you trying to ask me out? Really, you aren't my type. Even after a few beers." He chuckled to himself.

"Well, granted, I like people without dicks, so maybe I'd consider you after a few myself. But no. Actually, I exist now to destroy you."

At this moment, I received a lighting bolt of inspiration.

"Setting stuff on fire now, are we? I used to report on the War Memorial, Adam. You know that. Think this wouldn't come out?"

Adam's eyebrows shot up, so I thought I might be onto something.

"That's right, motherfucker. Someone knows about your little stunt. But you know what? I don't care about that. I care about the fact that you think you can do whatever you want to win. That you can squash the people you don't care about to get what you want. I'm not going to stand for that this semester, either. If you want to be student body president, you are going to have to fight for it. You and me. You know the Applied rooms you don't give a shit about? That's where all my fucks went to die. RIP, fucks! Watch your back, SGA boy. I'm running for president of Student Government." I turned and stormed away from him.

He just stood there, unable to speak.

Lacey later pointed out that we might have had an element of surprise on our side before the confrontation. That my outburst alerted him to my candidacy before I had even declared it.

"Although," she said, "have you considered writing poetry? You really do have a way with words."

Fuck me. That was one of the nicest things anyone's ever said.

Sincerely,

Brynn

Folder: Drafts
To: Rachel@msnbc.com
From: Brynnieh0401@gmail.com
Date: January 11
Subject: Sleeping and the Enemy

Dear Rachel Maddow,

Conversations like this have become the norm between Michaela and me:

"When are you going to get signatures? I'm pretty sure they are due really early. You need to check on that date."

"I know, I know. I will. Sarah said she'd check for me."

"So have you been talking to Sarah a lot lately?" Michaela's voice had a strange note in it.

"Not a *lot*," I said. "But some." I looked at her quizzically. "Does that bother you?"

"No."

"Really?"

"Maybe. A little," Michaela said.

"Why?" I said.

"Because I think she still likes you."

"She's with Nancy now."

"They broke up ages ago. I think Sarah talks about you in front of me to piss me off," said Michaela.

"We just have a common cause," I said.

"A common cause that she talked you into," she said.

"Technically it was Justin. And Thomas Jefferson."

"Sure."

"Okay. Sarah's there. I don't know. I don't still have a thing for her. I'm totally over her."

(Totally over. One hundred percent, ultra over. Even if she still talks about me. Except she wore this pleated skirt ensemble with her hair down today and of course I noticed. I mean, I'm only human, Rachel.)

"It's just the cause, then. Not because you still want to be with Sarah?" she said.

"No more exy-sexy times! I'm yours! Wait . . ." I said, realizing we were in fact having this conversation out loud. "Uh. I mean. Am I *officially* yours? Is this what this is about?"

Michaela picked a loose strand on her jeans. "I'd understand if you weren't interested."

"Not interested? Are you insane?"

She smiled. "Possibly."

"That's fine. Aren't we all? Listen, I'm all yours. It's just that Adam must be stopped."

"Okay, okay. Just don't sleep with Sarah?"

"Wasn't gonna." I shook my head.

Fortunately the bell rang and Michaela had to leave, ending this painful exchange.

Painful.

But! Girlfriend! I had a girlfriend!

I checked my phone at lunch, to notice that Sarah had texted. Nine times. I didn't even read them. But. What was this girl's game? Did Michaela know something I didn't? I clicked my phone off and looked out the window.

What did Sarah want with me now? Was she sorry she dumped me? Did I have potential again? Was I less drama? Yes and no.

Rachel, I don't want Sarah back. Not even a little. Because Michaela! Though Sarah was my girl first. My first. Everything, really.

Shit.

Sincerely,

Brynn

154

Folder: Drafts
To: Rachel@msnbc.com
From: Brynnieh0401@gmail.com
Date: January 14
Subject: Canvassing

Dear Rachel Maddow,

Before I even started to walk to school, I saw Sarah's car idling down the block from my house. I stopped and tapped on the window.

"There you are," she said. "Hop in."

"What?"

"I'll give you a ride. I have to talk to you."

Every cell in my body knew it should flee this scene, but every cell also didn't want to brave the ice and snow for three-quarters of a mile. And Sarah had her mom's car, which had heated seats.

"Okay," I said. Those damn seats felt like a hug.

"Signatures are due today," she said.

"What?"

"You have to declare your intent to run *by today*. Didn't you get my texts?"

"Uh . . ."

"Brynn, there is no way you forgot when you had to turn these things in. You are doing this on purpose."

"Well . . . ?"

"You have to get signatures in. Today," she said.

"But I haven't even started yet! Maybe Maynard will make an exception for me?" I said.

Sarah was right. The due date haunted my once-sexy dreams. I had kind of been hoping a signature fairy would collect names for me. Or another worthy candidate who wasn't me would magically appear and I wouldn't have to do this at all.

"Don't chance it, Brynn. This is Adam we are talking about."

"Okay, okay. You're right. I got it."

We pulled into the parking lot. Panic started to churn in my stomach.

"Do you want help?"

"No. It's okay. I got this."

I threw myself into the blue room. Mr. Grimm let me go around and everybody in the Color Coded Kingdom signed, so I was up to thirty-two already.

"How am I going to get any more?" I asked everyone at lunch. "My only friends are down here. Surely somebody down here has connections?"

Lacey chimed in. "I have spent the better part of my education trying to ignore most of the people on the floors above. But surely Greg or Riley could at least scare people into helping you during art. Or what about gym?"

I thought about that. One art classroom wasn't going to cut it. Nor was gym, where everyone except two jock girls spent the whole period trying to get out of whatever the gym teacher was trying to make us do that day. The only people I kind of knew were down here with me or possibly the younger siblings of Nick's loser crowd.

Although, losers *were* still matriculated. . . .

After school I made Michaela come with me to get names, so she could call 911 if I got shanked under the bleachers.

"Yo, bruh, why am I signing this shit now?"

I was arguing with a guy who was totally stoned and seemed to have been that way for the last fifteen years. He was a friend of a friend of a little brother to a friend of Nick.

"You know Student Government?" I said again.

"No, what is that?"

"We have kids who do stuff at the school. Likes dances and things."

"This is for a dance?"

"No," I said.

(Was this what Nick was like at the end? Did I repress this?)

"You have thoughts," I said. "You have feelings. You want a person who cares about you doing this thing that I explained to you like five times. Just sign the damn paper."

"Okay, fine. But only cause you're cute," he said.

I shuddered, but let it go because the dude signed the paper. This was the underside of politics. He had surprisingly beautiful penmanship. Michaela looked disgusted. I gave her a grateful smile.

Since the stoner guy signed, the other kids behind the bleachers signed, too. And because they signed, the guys having a smoke outside of the auto body classroom signed. And because I got auto body, the wood shop people signed. And because the wood shop people signed, the AV kids signed. Not the ones who ran the tiny radio station or the morning video announcements, mind you. But still the ones who ran the flat-screens and SMART Boards and shit to classrooms. And because I got all of them, I got some of the kids in the teen-parent trailer and some girls in the home ec cohort. And one of *those* girls was a cheerleader and she got half the squad who had stayed around for assisted stretching. *They* got some basketball players, even though two of them were Honors. They just agreed with my cause. And once you get basketball, you get anyone else who was left standing around waiting for a bus.

Some people signed because they *agreed* with my *cause*, Rachel.

Anyway, that was why, at 3:39 p.m., I found Mr. Maynard putting on his coat in the office, flailing my petitions at him. He looked a little alarmed as I rushed toward him, but he didn't try to hide behind the copier.

"Mr. Maynard," I gasped. "I have"—gasp—"the signatures." I thrust the names at him. All one hundred and eight of them.

He looked over my sheets. "Impressive, Ms. Harper. Very impressive. I had heard you might run. I'm pleased to see that you are. Ah. Yes. I know many of these names well." He chuckled darkly. "No detention without representation, I suppose."

I cocked my head at him.

"Sorry, sorry," he said. "Good work." He flipped open his really nice man bag and tucked them inside.

Michaela was waiting for me outside the office.

"I'm starving," I said to her.

Michaela laughed. "Me too. Canvassing is hard work."

"Is that what we were doing?"

"Yes, I think so. I have a feeling there will be more of it, if I stick with the likes of you." She poked me in my side.

"Ugh. Let's not think about that at the moment. One election at a time. Let's get cheese fries instead."

"That has my vote," she said.

I'd like to think you would be impressed, Rachel. This is only the beginning. Hopefully I'm doing my part for liberty and justice for all.

Sincerely,

Brynn

Folder:	Drafts
To:	Rachel@msnbc.com
From:	Brynnieh0401@gmail.com
Date:	January 15
Subject:	Applied Communications

Dear Rachel Maddow,

Now that I was officially in the race against Adam, the next step was to make a commercial. Sarah didn't need one, Justin didn't need one, the sophomore running for secretary didn't need one. Just the presidential candidates. Years ago a company had donated a slew of televisions for every classroom in the building. They were all wired to a central location so each homeroom could watch the company's show. I think it was a news program. It's a shame that ended before I got to ninth grade.

Now the TVs were used for announcements and the occasional shit-show Student Government campaign ads.

Mr. Grimm, citing something about applied pragmatism, gave over his class time to the new cause of Take Adam Down. This meant that Sarah and Justin came during their study hall to talk campaign commercial strategy.

"Wow," said Sarah, walking into the blue room. "I thought the boiler room was down here."

"I didn't know you were a comedian," I said, though she looked like she was serious.

"So what do we do?" asked Sarah and Justin in unison. Bianca, Riley, Greg, and Lance sat huddled in the corner, whispering behind their hands. I wished Michaela were there as a reinforcement, but she was out of school for the morning because of a dentist appointment.

"I have been researching political strategy," said Lacey, wheeling over.

"God, yes," Justin kind of half moaned.

I punched him in the arm because it felt like the right thing to do.

"We need to get people's attention. Because to most people Student

Government is just the kids against trays in the cafeteria and the jerks who got rid of snacks at the dances," said Lacey.

"It is not SGA's fault we had to get rid of the food at the dances. People were flushing bags of pretzels down the toilets. We were told we had to solve the problem," Sarah said.

Lacey shrugged. "Whatever. I'm just saying we need to make an impact here. I have some ideas, but I want to hear you brainstorm."

Mr. Grimm, who watched us from the desk at the front of the room, unfolded himself from the chair and moved the rolling whiteboard over to us. He handed me a dry-erase marker and winked.

"Okay. Go," Lacey said. We all stood there and looked at her.

"You should frame the commercial with an offer to donate a dollar to charity every time someone trips Adam in the cafeteria," chimed in Bianca.

It wasn't a bad idea. I wrote it on the board. "Harm Adam = $$." I grinned at Lacey.

"Encouraging assault is likely not the way to win the presidency, although I appreciate your creativity, Bee." Lacey sighed. "Also it's not unprecedented," she added. "What else?"

"We should make a zombie thriller staring Brynn," said Justin. "People love zombies."

"Zombie Brynn," I wrote on the board.

After an hour, we had the outline for a pretty offensive rap song about Adam, a fake debate with beagle puppies, me in my own soap opera, bribes to get people to vote, and blackmail.

"People," Lacey said. "You are not taking this seriously."

"We are!" I said. "I'm still rooting for the zombie movie. Put that sucker on the school televisions and website, let me go viral, and watch the votes roll in."

"Okay, fine. You are the candidate. If that's what you want, that's what you get."

Justin spoke up. "I know AV people. I got this, Lacey. Trust me."

"Fine," Lacey said. She did not look convinced. She rolled over to me. "Brynn."

"Uh-oh."

"No, listen." She wheeled as close to me as she could get. "We need polls in the field."

"What the ever living hell does that mean?" I played dumb.

Confession, Rachel: Of course I know what that shit means. There are like a zillion people running for stuff all of the time, and you are all over the polls with your bar graphs and shit.

"Knock it off, Brynn. You know what I mean. You are going to the people to find out their issues."

"Why me? Don't people usually have staffers to do this sort of thing? Make Justin do it. He's going to be in charge of the money. Make him earn it."

"You are the vox populi embodied."

"What does that even . . . oh, you know what? Forget it. Contextual clues." I shook my head as Mr. Grimm laughed from his desk. "Fine, give me a damn clipboard and I'll do whatever you want."

"I'll go with you," said Sarah suddenly.

My head snapped up.

"I'm running, too," she said. "I should know the issues."

Lacey raised her eyebrows. "Fine," she said after a particularly long pause. "I'll give you the list of questions I think you should ask. Please return all the data to me because I have a three-page reflection due this Saturday for class."

"Fine," I said.

"Fine," said Sarah.

Sincerely,

Brynn

Folder:	Drafts
To:	Rachel@msnbc.com
From:	Brynnieh0401@gmail.com
Date:	January 18
Subject:	Under where?

Dear Rachel Maddow,

I worked the register today at Aerie. I usually got out of that, as it was practically a full-time job keeping the freaking drawers and displays from looking like mythic groundhogs had burrowed through them for comfortable homes. The reg is boring, as hours pass with click, click, that'll be 39.99, click, click, have a nice day.

I had spent some time on this slow night staring at what appeared to be a lipstick stain on the counter. I was torn between bleaching the whole thing—because how the fuck did it get there?—or pretending that it didn't exist because *ew*. I was just about to search for some bleach wipes but someone approached.

"Sarah," I said, surprised.

"Brynn," she said, sounding equally surprised.

"Can I, uh, help you?" I said.

"No. Um. I wasn't shopping. I mean, I was. Not here. Not that I wouldn't shop here. I was just in the neighborhood and thought I'd stop by." She blushed. "I saw you in here the last time I was at the mall."

So she *had* seen me a few months ago. Universe, just kill me now.

"Oh. Okay." I stared at her.

"So." She cleared her throat again. "How have you been? Bikinis still on sale?"

"Uh. I'm fine. I guess. And suits aren't on sale, but I think we still have the ones you'd like in your size."

"I wasn't picked for Model UN camp in Pittsburgh."

"Oh?" I said. This was the first I'd heard of Sarah's interest in Model UN.

"Yeah. I have other choices, I guess. It just sucks because I really wanted it. They award two full scholarships to the state school of your choice. I could be a counselor at my summer camp. But it's not the same."

"Yeah," I said. "That sucks."

"Brynn," she said after a few moments. "I think I made a mistake. With us."

I just stared at her.

"And I just wondered . . . you know . . . if we . . ."

Here is where I wondered if I were dreaming, Rachel. Here was Sarah, wanting me back? Or maybe just needing comfort from good old Brynnie, who sure as hell wasn't going anywhere. Sarah looked so sad and dejected.

"What about Nancy?" I said.

"Oh, man. Well, you know, she turned eighteen in October. And she didn't even vote. *And* I found out that she helped her mom canvass in the last presidential election. She went door to door. *For the Republican candidate.*"

"That's horrible," I sympathized.

Sarah smiled. "Listen, you don't have to say anything now. Just think about it."

Oh, I do have to say something now. I do I do I do I do. Because Michaela would not be pleased with this. And what? What was even happening with Sarah right now?

"Okay," my mouth answered for me. "Do you want to see the one I thought you'd like? You'll need one for summer camp." My brain slapped my tongue so hard I flinched.

"Okay." She smiled bigger.

I was right. She loved the stupid two-piece, sexy-as-hell crap so much that she squeezed my arm just like she used to. I rang her out with my discount.

"Who was that?" Erin asked after Sarah left. "Is that your girlfriend who you keep talking about?"

"Not exactly," I said. I ran away from her before she could ask more questions.

I wanted to hide under the counter and maybe curl up and die, but there appeared to be lipstick on the floor.

Sincerely,

Brynn

Folder: Drafts
To: Rachel@msnbc.com
From: Brynnieh0401@gmail.com
Date: January 23
Subject: In the Field

Dear Rachel Maddow,

Bless you for talking to people *for a living*. People suck.

"Listen, I'm trying to help you," I said to a guy whose face was completely covered by his hair.

"You don't know me. I don't need help," he said.

Goth and Emo married and birthed this dude.

I was under the bleachers again, this time vox populi–ing.

"Elections affect us all!" I tried again. "Even the small ones. Just answer the fucking question!"

"Um," said Sarah, holding the clipboard.

"Shut it," I told her. She was out of her element. This was *my* constituency. "Motherfucker, just tell me how you feel about the food in the cafeteria."

"It sucks," said Gothmo.

"But *why*?" I said.

"They are always out of ketchup. And the peas are gray."

"Gray peas. No ketchup. Got it. See? These are concrete examples of things that can be addressed. Don't you want a student body president who will bring these concerns to the administration? Vote for me! Say no to gray peas!"

"What's your name again?" he said.

"Oh, Jesus. Just take the sticker." I slapped a newly Justin-designed zombie Brynn on the guy's weathered black collar. "There will be nachos at the polls. March 19. Bring your student ID. For the love of holy fuckballs, vote, okay?"

"Nachos. Cool," he said.

I banged my head on my clipboard as I walked away.

"Um . . ." Sarah said again.

I glared at her.

"I was just going to say good job," she said, raising her hands and laughing.

"You were not. I know that look. You were going to tell me to be nicer."

"Maybe. That doesn't change the fact that you are doing a good job." She smiled. We'd been doing this together for three days. I made sure to text Michaela for a solid hour each night to tell her every last thing that happened (maybe omitting how much time I'd been spending with Sarah). Also though, completely by accident, I still hadn't told Sarah *no way were we ever going to be a couple again*, which I knew I should have. I was hoping she'd realize I was the same person, same drama, and give up the idea herself. I wasn't usually so averse to confrontation, but she'd been wearing her skinny jeans and have I mentioned I'm only human?

We marched across the field to the pep band. We'd had a week of weather in the fifty-degree range and the snow was basically gone. The band, which won way more titles than the football team, enthused all over the damp grass.

"Excuse me," I called to the drummers. They seemed the most likely to get me. "I need to talk to you about issues!"

Sarah trailed behind, recording their answers.

"We practice in a bathroom. In a literal bathroom. There are urinals," said a band kid.

"Shut up," I said.

"Dead serious. It's under the stage where you would wait before going up to perform. But I sit next to a urinal." She wrinkled her nose.

"At least you aren't back with the toxic mold!" yelled a trombone.

"Don't get me started about the leaking tiles," said a trumpet.

"And we need new instruments," said a flute.

I dutifully spoke with each band member. They were way more

receptive than the bleacher crowd, though similarly concerned with no ketchup and gray peas. I handed out Brynn zombie stickers. "Be sure to vote," I said. "Nachos! March 19! Bring your student ID! Vote for Brynn! Band kids are good in bed!" I yelled.

That got a cheer from them and an eye roll from Sarah.

Sincerely,

Brynn

Folder: Drafts
To: Rachel@msnbc.com
From: Brynnieh0401@gmail.com
Date: January 25
Subject: Moves and Countermoves

Dear Rachel Maddow,

Nick was a chess player. He tried to teach me, and there was a point that I got pretty good even though I was ten. But I went to a vicious place in my mind to win, and it freaked me the fuck out. He lost interest (or the brain cells), so I hadn't played in years. But it felt very much like I was a rook in my own life. Someone would move me forward, someone else would advance his piece, I would retreat unbidden, picked up and set down by an unseen hand. If only Nick were here to give me a refresher course, because I don't remember what direction to send all the other pieces if I want to win.

On the campaign front, Adam had been keeping a pretty low profile. He was riding the wrestling-star cred into non-action. But I guess someone clued him in to the fable of the tortoise and the hare. With my appeal to the loser demographic (which, it appeared, made up much of the school), I was gaining on him as Ms. Vox Popularity. I should have known that would piss him off.

Today after the morning announcements, Mr. Maynard aired our campaign commercials. I was kind of nervous, because I hadn't actually been involved in making it. Justin felt it was better left a surprise. After Nancy wished us a good start to our weekend on the morning video announcements, the screens flickered blue for a moment.

Then the television wavered again to show two dudes. One was . . . well, actually no, one was a girl. Only not. She looked like she had some kind of skin disease. With big, puffy hair and this huge ass and a shirt that read "Brynn" and, oh, of course, it was me. I looked over at Lacey.

"This isn't your commercial," she said. "I saw what Justin did. This must be Adam's."

The other dude on screen was clean-cut to the point where I thought he could work at Aerie. He would look better in the cheekies than I would. Kid must work out, because he could almost make me consider bi-curiosity. (Almost.) Then they started speaking.

"Hey, Brynn."

"Hey, Adam."

"What are you doing running for SGA president?"

"Well," he/she snorted, "I thought it would get me some . . ."

"Influence?"

"No!" Giggle. Snort.

"Opportunities to enact change?"

"No!"

"Then what?"

"Extra credit!" Snort, laugh, etc.

The screen clicked off. I rolled my eyes. Honestly, what was Adam's problem? Was he saying I was too stupid to be student body president? That I was less because I was in Applied? That looked to be what Lance, Bianca, Riley, and Greg thought he meant because they all looked pretty pissed.

But *then*. The screens flicked to life again. The perspective of the camera looked like a video game—like someone had a camera attached to her head. The person crunched through grass and leaves, as if in the woods. Little filtered through the lens, just darkness and sometimes a branch. But then a scream pierced through the crappy school-wide speaker system. A pale . . . zombie . . . crashed into the frame and grabbed the camera (or presumably the face of the person walking).

"Help me, Adam," a voice gasped.

Another male scream erupted then. "Adam, Adam, noooooo."

Blood splashed the camera. Or, hopefully, ketchup. But then someone loomed over the camera. A puffy-haired girl. I ran my hand over my head. (My wavy hair got frizzy in humidity, but was that seriously my defining feature?) The character *looked* like me, but I couldn't quite make me out. "I" wiped blood off the lens.

"It's going to be okay," my doppelgänger said as she kicked the air violently.

A wrenching gasp escaped from the pale thing. It collapsed to the ground out of the shot.

"I won't leave you when times get tough," "I" said.

"Thank you, Brynn," the camera wearer sighed.

The screens flicked off.

The blue room burst into cheers. Justin and the AV crew were officially the Patron Saints of Epic.

Lacey told me her aide was in the office and witnessed Adam getting yelled at. Maynard was *not* happy about his ad and had yanked it seconds after it got mean. Apparently it went on for another minute like that. School elections had managed to run for years without a smear campaign, but leave it to Adam to fuck it up. Because of his dick move, there would be no more commercials (they were supposed to run all next week, too). Next year, ads will have to be reviewed, if they are allowed at all. But I got several more nods from people in the hallway than before. So I'm calling it a success.

Youth political involvement is not dead, Rachel. It is seriously, seriously, undead.

Sincerely,

Brynn

Folder: Sent
To: mmaynard@westing.pa.edu
From: JSG@GraffHunterWexley.net
Date: January 27
Subject: RE:

Dear Principal Maynard,

I am in receipt of your concerns. I take issue with the implication that Adam had anything to do with that campaign ad. His friends insisted on putting it together for him. He did not view it and was under the impression it was not to be aired until next week. Had he seen it in advance, he has assured me he would have pulled it and had it redone over this Saturday and Sunday.

However, I have viewed the content myself and honestly don't see what is wrong with it. It spoofs the appearance of Adam's opponent, but not in an overly cruel way. I have been led to believe that the young lady actually resembles the woman in the film. Furthermore, the satire used is accurate. The school *does* deserve a president who holds himself to high academic and social standards.

I trust you will continue to work for the interest of all students, and consider no further punishment toward Adam or his team. I'm told the recent donations to the school library from my corporation have already aided students.

Sincerely,

Jonathan S. Graff, Esquire

Folder:	Drafts
To:	Rachel@msnbc.com
From:	Brynnieh0401@gmail.com
Date:	January 30
Subject:	Debate Prep

Dear Rachel Maddow,

I had a dream about you last night. It was the first one you've starred in, even though I've been watching you these many years. My sleeping brain isn't usually that deep. I most often dream I have to pee but can't find a bathroom, or find a toilet but it's out in the open or really gross or something. Sometimes I dream about Michaela. Or, more often I'm sad to say, Sarah. We're at her house and everything seems normal, like we never broke up. Neither of us mentions the weirdness of the past months. I keep wondering if she'll say something, but then she doesn't. And sometimes Nick visits me. He's always pretty messed up on something. That's how I remember him best. The sadness of that fills me from toes to heart.

In your dream, I was a guest on your show with Michaela. She told some story about her life, and you were sympathetic. I mostly goofed around, and you and I got into a giggling fit that was inappropriate given whatever elected official you were about to interview. It was a ridiculous thing that could never happen, but I woke up happy.

My good mood held even though I saw Adam in the hallway again. He *literally* sneered at me, but I ignored him. In the blue room, Lacey and company took over. She had Justin cram the white board with tiny red print. "Cafeteria concerns," reads one column. "Student programming budgets," read another. I saw Sarah's notes from my vox populi–ing neatly outlined.

"Ask me anything," I said to Justin. Sarah handed him some index cards so we could prep for the debate next week. It would be in a town hall sort of meeting. Anyone could ask questions from the audience. This had its pros and cons.

Mostly cons.

I took my place up front. Lacey lined up Bianca and company to observe. They sat with my campaign team. Sarah nervously perched on the edge of her seat.

"Brynn." Justin eyed me. "What are your thoughts on gray peas?"

"While I understand it is difficult to cook for hundreds of different students, many of whom have specific dietary needs." I looked down at my notes. "I also contend that lunches may be nutritious and delicious. I propose forming a student advisory committee to work with the cafeteria staff to uphold governmental guidelines while finding creative culinary solutions." I waited a beat. "A vote for me is a vote against gray peas!"

Bianca and the others cheered.

"Ms. Harper," started Sarah, "I had heard it alleged that you are running for this position because you are angry about the censorship of the student paper. You do realize no one *reads* the student paper, right?" I could tell that startled Justin. A look of betrayal crossed his face before he composed himself.

"There have been certain new restrictions imposed on the student paper recently. Administration has invoked their right to read all content before it is published. That has led to a new direction for a class and club I had at one point considered a second family. However, as with all change, there are opportunities for growth and expansion and increased readership. Now we can move more into the digital age."

The rest of the day flew by. Ms. Yee shooed everyone out for her classes, but by then it was obvious that I was ready.

"You have a one-liner for everything?" Sarah asked me afterward.

"Just about," I sighed. "Sound bites. You know."

"Aren't you underestimating your voters?"

"Sarah . . ." I cocked my head at her. "You've met me, no? *I'm* a voter."

"Fair enough." She smiled. "You ready for this?"

"Ready as I'll ever be."

Wish you could be there to see this, Rachel, liberty and justice for all. Well. Shmiberty and shmustus, anyway. I could go on your show and we could do a point-by-point analysis. One day, maybe.

Sincerely,

Brynn

Folder: Drafts
To: Rachel@msnbc.com
From: Brynnieh0401@gmail.com
Date: February 2
Subject: The first family

Dear Rachel Maddow,

I convinced Michaela to walk around down by the War Memorial with me. I snapped pictures of fraying caution tape waving in the wind and of the tarps flapping around, now doing little to protect what was left from winter weather. The city still didn't have enough money to repair it. A committee formed to find donors, and they were doing okay. So much had already gone out of Westing. This place, which held concerts and hockey games and high school graduations, was one of the last points of pride Westing had. People wanted to save it.

I kicked around stones in the parking lot. They wedged in dirty snowbanks, melting ice mingling with oil to make rainbows. I remembered when Nick would bring me here to play on the "ice mountains." Snowplows brought much of the downtown snow here, so the piles reached over my head, even now. They'd found Nick's body not far from here. I wondered what he thought, as he died. Did he remember we used to laugh and try to sneak snow down each other's backs?

"You really think Adam did this?" Michaela asked, interrupting my thoughts.

"Who knows? It's a real shame, no matter who did it," I said.

"Yeah," said Michaela. She rubbed the dark circles under her eyes.

"You okay?" I asked. These days all I talked about were zombies and political opponents. I wondered if she somehow felt the sadness of the abandoned lot.

"I'm just tired," she said. "Grandma has started yelling at night. She calls out for people I don't know. My uncle works eleven to seven, so I'm in charge of her when he's not there. It was fine, but now she yells."

"I'm sorry. Could I help, somehow?"

"No. I don't think so." She looked out into the orange water flowing in the pale concrete riverbed beyond the parking lot.

"Hey. Come here," I said. I wrapped my arms around her. She put her face in my hair.

We stood like that for a long time, hidden by the charred remains of Westing's dignity. Eventually we got cold and went home. Her to her grandmother, me to Mom's rage that I forgot to shut the back door firmly and leaked expensive heat all day. I offered to pay her back just to make her stop yelling. She just gave me a disgusted look, but after she went to put laundry in the dryer, Fart Weasel grabbed the twenty that I'd waved in Mom's face. That made me feel icky and gross, and I needed to not feel that way immediately or I was going to barf.

"Hey," I texted Michaela.

"Hey," she said.

"You know what?"

"What?"

"You're awesome. For taking care of your gram. I don't know why you had to move here, but I'm glad you did."

"I'm not that good at it. Taking care of her."

"It's hard," I said.

I stared at the infuriating blinking dots.

"I'm glad I moved here, too."

I grinned. "Did I tell you about the new Aerie tank tops?"

"Brynn Harper, I'm in pain, are you going to start sending dirty texts?"

"I was planning on it, yes."

"Good."

I don't know if I was the best at cheering Michaela up, but she seemed in much better spirits. Sometimes when things are falling apart, you can't rebuild. And sometimes, maybe you can.

Sincerely,
Brynn

Folder:	Drafts
To:	Rachel@msnbc.com
From:	Brynnieh0401@gmail.com
Date:	February 6
Subject:	Debatable Debacle

Dear Rachel Maddow,

I tossed and turned so much that I gave up trying to sleep because I was worried I'd strangle myself in the covers. My brain wouldn't quit so I got up to lay it all on you, Rachel.

Today I was not myself. I was better. I was on Brynn overdrive. Mr. Maynard was a "moderator" and had starter questions for us before the audience could chime in from the town hall.

"Ms. Harper, what are your thoughts on cafeteria food?" Maynard started with an easy question. I had won the coin toss, so I got to answer first.

I went into my prepared response.

"A vote for me is a vote against gray peas," I finished triumphantly.

The audience cheered.

"I hope to get outside vendors to cater lunch at least once a week!"

The audience roared for Adam, as if what he proposed could ever find funding.

"All students need to be represented equally. I will listen to your opinions, and even if I hate you and you hate me, I will still try to get your shit on the table. I mean, issues. Issues on the table." Mr. Maynard hadn't even tried to bleep my answer.

The audience cheered for me once again.

"I will come to your club meetings and homerooms. I will dance with you at homecoming and get you punch at the prom. I'm just this guy who wants to be your friend. And if we get some cool stuff done, that's great, too, you know?" Adam grinned at the world.

He was one toothy motherfucker.

"I'll get the band out of the basement," I'd answer.

"The band is in the basement?" Adam honestly sounded confused.

(Score one for Brynn.)

"I'll . . . uh . . . what's wrong with the football padding again?" I said, in answer to an athletics question.

"There is a reason cheerleaders and boosters and the band and everyone comes to see you on a Friday night. It's because you're the best thing this town has ever seen. You're going to go to state, and, damn it, you are going to go with new helmets and the best gear available!" Adam threw a thumbs-up to his fellow athletes.

(Score one for Adam.)

Adam played his part well, the slime mold ball sack. That kid *is* probably going to be in politics one day. That's enough to make a girl like me study harder so that I can prepare to defeat him. For every pithy thing I said, Adam pithed back. There was a lot of cheering as both of us seemed to agree on the importance of adequate ketchup availability. The final minutes were ticking down. Adam and I glared at each other when Maynard asked for any final questions from the audience.

Michaela rose from her chair and took the microphone in the middle of the room.

There was a moment of silence as eyes and faces shifted toward her. Someone whooped for her in the back.

"This question is for Adam," Michaela said. "If elected, how will you make sure to represent the interests of the entire student body and not just those of your own social group?"

God, how I loved that girl in that moment.

"I promise to do everything I can for all of the voters. I know that I will need to forge my own path," he said. "I pledge allegiance to Westing High, and to God and country!"

Legit, he actually said that, God and country.

"Right, but how?" she said.

"I will continue to work for the betterment of all students," he said.

"You still didn't answer the question."

"I believe I did."

"Um. No. I would like you to at least say how you will pledge allegiance to issues other than your own."

A stir circled around the crowd.

"I can tell you how *I* would represent everyone," I offered.

"Why don't we give Mr. Graff a chance, Ms. Harper," Mr. Maynard said. "The question was for him."

I looked at Adam. "So, if you are elected the SGA president, how *will* this be about the students and not about you?"

Adam grimaced. "I answered the question," he said. Was he choking? Or did he just not have anything to say? Adam had bragged that he hadn't prepped, like it was a point of pride to just wing it. It seemed the strategy had backfired.

Mr. Maynard looked at Adam for a few seconds longer, waiting to see if he was going to say anything else. When Adam remained silent, Mr. Maynard said, "Ms. Harper? Your thoughts?"

"Well, I would represent the students of Westing by talking to as many of you as possible. Making your concerns my concerns. No one group would be treated differently from any other. One Westing!" I shouted.

"One Westing, one Westing!" Justin started shouting. Sarah joined in, and soon the whole room cheered like the football team just stage dove into the crowd.

Mr. Maynard concluded the debate. Adam stalked off, clearly furious.

"What the hell was that?" asked Justin when we all made it back to the blue room. "Beautiful!"

I smiled.

"You know," said Lacey, rolling in, "it's generally demonstrated that politics are in fact about hate, not love. People will vote because they hate the other candidate, not because they love their own. In the absence of parties, per se, the same behavior arises. People align with a candidate not because of positions *for* issues, but because of feelings *against* others. Somehow, Brynn, you managed to appeal to both. I'm proud of you."

"We'll see," said Justin.

I left the school on my way to work, pleased with everything. The general consensus seemed to be that I had pummeled Adam. If nothing else, I had made Lacey proud again. I walked down the sidewalk thinking how someday she'd be famous, and I could use her as a second reference on my application for an Aerie management position.

Sincerely,
Brynn

Folder: Drafts
To: Rachel@msnbc.com
From: Brynnieh0401@gmail.com
Date: February 11
Subject: Bleak midwinter

Dear Rachel Maddow,

Campaigning is going well. Off the success of the debate, Sarah commissioned the graphic designers on yearbook to make "Applied Pride" buttons and stickers. All of us handed them out to anyone who couldn't get away fast enough. I liked them better than the "Brynn for the Win" e-mail Justin spammed to everybody he knew online. I was daydreaming about fundraising to make my own T-shirts as I walked up the stairs at the end of the day. I stopped short, a gaggle of people blocking the doors.

"What's going on?" I asked.

A kid I knew from Music Appreciation looked at me. "Um," he said.

The entire hallway had been wallpapered. I inspected a section of flyer-plastered cinder block.

"Brynn Harper is gay," I read out loud. On it was an awful picture of me from I think tenth grade. (Guess Adam still had access to the yearbook files.)

"Brynn Harper hasn't APPLIED herself and will FLUNK forever," I read on another. *That* poster had a picture of me passed out on someone's couch with a book on my chest. The irony was that that was from when I was a good student and had just fallen asleep at Adam's house studying. Bet Adam himself might have snapped that when we still hung out. Prick.

"Brynn Harper sucks dick," I read. I stood in front of it for a minute. Someone sneezed next to me. I looked over. Two or three of my Westing High constituents stood looking at me. I cleared my throat. "I mean, which is it?" I asked them, and four more people who stopped. "Do I suck dick, or am I gay?" I sucked in my breath. "Or maybe this is implying I'm bi?" I chuckled. "Yeah, no, I'm just a lesbian." I ripped down the "Brynn Harper sucks dick" sign. And another one. And another and another and another. Chunks of wall stuck out, red against the white meanness I left up. "There. That's more accurate." I left up the lesbian signs and nodded at the wall in satisfaction.

The still-gathering crowd watched me do all this. Then one person started clapping. The kid next to her joined in, and soon everyone was chanting my name. "Brynn, Brynn, Brynn!" they shouted. I bowed instinctively, like when I was a flower in my second-grade play.

Breaking headline: I am a lesbian. I am not flunking at the moment because of Mr. Grimm and Ms. Yee and Lacey and now Michaela. So that other attack was just a lie. If this was what Adam thought would get to me, he was wrong. As I tried to leave the crowd and make for the exit at the other end of the building, Michaela threw elbows to maneuver around bodies to get to me.

"Don't go this way," she said.

"It's okay. I've seen all these," I said, waving my hand at the posters.

"No. There are more. Turn around," she said.

"The lame Brynn sucks ones? Meh," I said.

Michaela rushed in front of me. "No. They are different. Still lame. So. Why don't you wait until someone takes them down?"

I leaned in and kissed her cheek. "How bad could they be? They are flyers. Flyers at least aren't the Internet." Michaela flinched a little at "Internet," but I caught her lips this time. I then faked a left with Michaela to see if she'd follow.

"Brynn, seriously . . ."

I stopped short, immediately regretting that I hadn't listened to her. On the far wall past the banks of lockers were several huge collages of Nick. Nick as a little boy with his guitar. Nick with his beloved, wretched Ford Pinto. Nick holding a knife to some kid's throat. I'd never seen that one before. Adam must have gotten these all online.

"Brynn Harper's hero," it said in large black letters.

Worse still was "She's just like him."

My mouth hung open, my feet rooted to the spot.

"I'm sorry," whispered Michaela from behind me. "They are foam board and superglued to the wall, and I couldn't get any of them down. Is that your brother?"

I turned and nodded at her. I moved my mouth, but no sounds came out. She squeezed my hand. People rushed in and around me, stopping to stare, stopping to stare at me staring. Most of them probably didn't even know who he was. Then Mr. Bill showed up. He took out what I swear to God was a machete and hacked the things to bits.

Moving on their own accord, my legs took me next to him.

"Gonna need the industrial solvent," he muttered to himself. Still I stood, staring at now confetti'ed Nick.

Nick.

That one with the guitar. That killed. I wasn't born yet. He was so happy. By the time I was aware of it, he could play more songs than I could even count.

Nick with a knife. Nick passed out. Nick, Nick, fucking Nick.

Guess Adam did know how to get to me after all.

Mr. Maynard pushed his way through the noisy bodies toward Mr. Bill. "All right, people, enough. *Enough,*" he shouted.

Everyone quickly dispersed. He looked at the walls. "The whole first floor is like this," he said. "Did you do this, Brynn?"

I looked at him, shocked. "You think *I* put these up?" I said, aghast.

"No," he said. "I just . . ." He put his hand on the back of his head, staring at the wall. "They cheered for you. I'm sorry. I didn't realize. I thought it might be like the underwear again. We'll get this cleaned up and find out who is responsible."

"I can tell you who is responsible, Mr. Maynard."

"Let's not jump to conclusions, Brynn."

I shrugged. "You can leave it up. I don't care."

Oh, fuck me, how I wished that were true.

You know what, Rachel? There are a lot of people who screw up on your show. Like, governors (or mayors or senators) who take bribes, or have affairs, or do really crazy shit with porn even here in Pennsylvania, where you'd think the only thing to report on is the dairy industry. But some of them . . . I wonder now if some of them are just regular people. Normal, everyday people who got pissed off or fired up or felt something that made them run for office to try to do something good. But then they weren't perfect in their lives before and stuff came up and other people used it against them. And then you reported it because it was news. Which I would do, too. Because don't people have the right to know?

I guess it all depends on your perspective.

Sincerely,
Brynn

Folder:	Sent
To:	mmaynard@westing.pa.edu
From:	JSG@GraffHunterWexley.net
Date:	February 12
Subject:	RE:

Dear Principal Maynard,

I am vexed by your last correspondence. Are you seriously considering the misguided claims as true? Pictures or no pictures, there is no way Adam was Involved In a prank like that. No way at all. And I assure you, I will confirm this is the case as swiftly as possible.

Sincerely,

Jonathan S. Graff, Esquire

Folder: Drafts
To: Rachel@msnbc.com
From: Brynnieh0401@gmail.com
Date: February 14
Subject: Don't leap

Dear Rachel Maddow,

The school was still abuzz after the hallway incident. Adam denied it, of course. Turns out the cameras monitoring the main hallway were fake, just to trick us into behaving or some shit.

"I could issue a statement," I said to Lacey at an emergency strategy session.

"To whom? Where? No. Let. It. Go," she said.

"Don't touch it. Run, don't walk away from this," Justin said.

"I agree with Lacey, don't touch it," Sarah said. She walked out with me after school.

Before I could argue, Sarah interrupted.

"I got into Westing State's summer junior senate program. So I'll be around!"

"That's great," I said.

"Yeah," she said. "It's not Model UN, but at least I won't have to stay in a dorm. And I don't know if I want to hang out with little kids all vacation, you know?"

"Ah," I said. "Well, I should go."

"Listen, Brynn. I'm sorry about last summer. I had a lot of stuff going on, and I freaked out. I'm really sorry, okay? I just lost track of myself."

I turned away from her. "Things weren't exactly peachy with me."

"I know." She stepped closer to me. "I'm sorry."

"Sarah. This would have been great months ago. But now? Why now?" I should have backed up. I should have run for my life.

"I just realized I was wrong, okay? I've had a lot of time to think. And you were right, a while ago, when you said I changed. And I was wrong when I said you didn't." She stepped even closer, putting a hand on my waist. "It's Valentine's Day."

"Sarah . . ." I breathed her in. I had always loved stupid Valentine's Day.

"Remember what we were like? You and I?" she whispered.

I did. Remember. The smell of her perfume. The brush of her eyelashes against my skin. I let her kiss my neck. I remembered that, too. It felt good. But also wrong.

"I have to go," I said.

"Okay," said Sarah. I could tell she was trying to read my face. But I doubt she had any more idea what I was feeling than I did.

I texted Michaela. "Do you want to do anything for V-Day?"

"LOL. Nah. It's a terrible holiday. So fake."

"Totally," I texted back.

I sat at home listening to Mom and Fart Weasel argue about whether to go to Al's Steakhouse or Bob's Butchery. At least I had the house to myself after they went with Bob's. I texted Michaela again, saying that she could come over if she wanted. No response. I figured her gram might be having trouble.

Maybe I should text Sarah.

Maybe not.

Sincerely,

Brynn

Folder: Drafts
To: Rachel@msnbc.com
From: Brynnieh0401@gmail.com
Date: February 19
Subject: Fishing .

Dear Rachel Maddow,

One month till the election. We aren't allowed to campaign anymore after the hallway incident. I can't even pass out my "Applied Pride" stickers. Lacey was disgruntled because she didn't want to use the "attack on Brynn and Nick" for her community college class project. I got my grades. Three As, and the rest Bs. It was a February miracle. It also inched me on the brink of being allowed back on the paper. I took lunch to go find Mr. McCloud to see if he'd let me back on with a few hundredths to go.

Mr. Maynard stopped me as I passed the main office. "Ms. Harper, wait. I need to speak to you for a second." His face looked somber.

I followed him to his office, where Adam was sitting, waiting for us. Maynard waved me into a seat next to Adam.

"Listen, you two," he said. "I need you to keep this civil. The attack on Brynn was unacceptable. But so is this."

"What?" I asked.

"Oh, don't play stupid. . . ." Adam said.

"Is this still about the debate? Look, isn't that what debates are for? It's not my fault you weren't prepared. . . ."

"This is not about the question," Adam growled. "You know what this is about."

I looked from Adam, to Mr. Maynard, back to Adam.

"Uh, noooo, I really don't."

"So you didn't e-mail the whole school pictures of me and Anderson?"

"Anderson? What?" I wasn't even trying to play dumb. I had zero idea what he was talking about. I gave a bewildered look to Mr. Maynard.

Maynard regarded me for a long moment but didn't say anything. "Can you bring up your school e-mail on my computer?" he asked.

"Okay?" I said. I gave Adam one more quizzical look before getting up and leaning over Mr. Maynard's keyboard. I never used my school e-mail. I logged in and then backed away from the desk.

"May I?" asked Mr. Maynard, gesturing to his screen.

"Sure," I said. All it had in it were cafeteria menus and the announcements we heard every day at school.

Mr. Maynard clicked around as I sat next to Adam. Mr. Maynard looked more and more upset. He swung the computer monitor toward us.

"Do you mind explaining this?" he said.

It took me a minute to figure out what I was looking at. To my horror, I realized that there was an e-mail in my outbox, sent to "All," with several screenshots of Adam next to the War Memorial Arena downtown pasted in the body of the letter. It was dark, but it was clearly him, with another kid (Anderson) I recognized from the student athlete display near the gym. There might have been more people there, but they could have just as well been shadows in the background.

In several pictures, Adam appeared to be lighting something. Firecrackers. In the last one, Adam was a blur running, a stupid big-ass grin on his face. The rest of the pictures were streaks of light . . . maybe flames.

So did this mean Adam really *did* cause the fire to the War Memorial? The news said just yesterday it was *still* under investigation, but no one was ever charged as far as I knew.

Holy Space God slimeball free-speech-and-voter-suppressing asshole. I hoped this wouldn't make people vote for me. It would be lame if Adam went down in flames like that. (HA!) (No but really.)

"Mr. Maynard. I know how this looks. I really do. But I *didn't* send those pictures."

"Of course she did," said Adam. Gone was the bravado. He seemed close to tears. "To get back at me for that hallway thing. Which *wasn't* me. I don't control people who want me to win. She threatened me that if I tried to be student body president, she would do this exact thing."

My jaw dropped. "I did *not*."

"You did."

"All right, all right. Both of you. Enough. You can go. But this isn't over."

Adam and I got up and left. I ran away from him downstairs to the blue room as fast as I could.

"You okay, Brynn?" asked Mr. Grimm. All I could was shake my head. How did Adam hack into my account? What was Adam's game, sending pictures of himself to the whole school?

And if it wasn't Adam who sent them, then who was it?

Sincerely,

Brynn

Folder: Sent
To: mmaynard@westing.pa.edu
From: JSG@GraffHunterWexley.net
Date: February 21
Subject: Further steps

Dear Principal Maynard,

It has come to my attention that there may be some merit to the claims of Adam's involvement in the unfortunate incident at the War Memorial.

I think we both know that boys will be boys. I think Adam's academic boredom with the Westing High curriculum might have contributed to his youthful antics.

We are willing to fully cooperate with the school and local authorities in this matter. As it happens, Adam feels he has further information about the events of the evening in question that will prove useful for the investigation. He did not want to come forward before because he did not want to get his friends (who were the *actual* perpetrators) in trouble. I have helped him come to see that it is time to do the right thing.

I would also like to discuss the matter of certain other parties who have recently taken it upon themselves to ruin my son's fine reputation. This is of the utmost concern to me.

Please feel free to schedule a meeting with my secretary as soon as possible.

Sincerely,
Jonathan S. Graff, Esquire

Folder:	Drafts
To:	Rachel@msnbc.com
From:	Brynnieh0401@gmail.com
Date:	February 22
Subject:	The hits just keep on coming

Dear Rachel Maddow,

I didn't even make it to class today. I had plans to ask Michaela to the movies as soon as she got to the blue room for peer tutoring. Instead, I was pulled into Maynard's House of Pain and Suffering before the first bell. My mom and Fart Weasel sat in the chairs in front of his desk. I sat, stunned.

"Brynn, I imagine you know why I called your parents in."

"Parent," I corrected him. "And the man married to her."

"Stop with your mouth, young lady," said Fart Wesel. The smell of awful rose off of him like skunk spray. "You see what we deal with," he said to Mr. Maynard.

Mr. Maynard looked curiously from them to me. "Yes, well, Brynn, I've invited them in today to talk about the accusation of libel and harassment that has been leveled against you."

"What?" I asked, surprised out of my stupor. "By whom?"

"By Adam Graff . . . and family," said Mr. Maynard tiredly.

"Oh my Sp . . . God, Mr. Maynard, honestly. *He* accused *me* of harassing him? Are you kidding? After that thing in the hallway? And I'm the one in here again?"

"More pictures of Mr. Graff went out last night. And they were sent from your school e-mail account. Again. And Mr. Graff has alleged that you might have put up the posters about yourself." Mr. Maynard looked pained listing the accusations against me.

"My . . . what? My e-mail?" I said. "I have barely used that. Ever. I sure as hell didn't send anything about *Adam*. Despite what almost everyone might think, I'm not *that* stupid. If you told me about it once, why would

I do it again from my own account?" Holy fucks why didn't I change my fucking password on Tuesday?

Probably because I never actually *send* e-mail from my school account.

"Well, we are investigating that. You were making such improvements in your academics, so I thought I should involve your parents. To help keep you on the right track."

"Oh, Mr. Maynard. You think my 'parents' give a shit?" I said, slumping back in my chair.

"You will not use language like that in front of a teacher!" Fart Weasel bellowed.

"Sir, I'm actually an administrator . . ." Mr. Maynard interrupted, but no one could compete with Fart when he got going.

"You chose to disrespect your mother and I one too many times with this. You are exactly like your brother. Exactly. Only, on my watch that shit isn't going to fly. You are coming home with us and you will stay there. You can go to school and that is it. If you so much as try to set a toe outside our place in that time, I will call the police and have you arrested, do you understand?"

"Why do you care? Is it just because the school called you in? Listen . . ."

The Fart was not finished. "You will stop talking. You are always talking. Just stop. You are coming with us even if you refuse to be helped." The vein on the back of his neck was bulging, he was trying so hard not to completely lose his shit in front of the principal.

Mr. Maynard, for his part, looked as though he completely regretted having called them. "Brynn," he said gently. "Perhaps some time at home to think about—"

"Thank you," said my mom. "That is enough. Please let us know if you need anything for the investigation. We are going to take her home to address these things as a family." Wow. She *could* speak. Who knew? She got up and grabbed my arm. She pushed me out the door. Fart Weasel followed too closely behind. Mom shoved me in their car. It smelled like cat litter.

"I can't believe you put me through that," she said. "After your brother . . ."

"How did you think you'd get away with fucking with that boy? What? Did he fuck you and leave you? Couldn't just leave it alone? We have to live in this town, too, you know."

This was the best he could do. Turning this back around to be about him. Anger flared up in my stomach, but as I stared out the car window, I felt cool and numb and removed from the whole thing. It was like I was watching a movie from the far back of the theater.

"I didn't do it, you know," I said mostly to Mom. "I have no idea who is doing what with those pictures."

"How did you know they were pictures?" she said. "If you didn't do it?"

"Well, like Mr. Maynard said a minute ago . . ."

"Enough. You've said enough. Just shut up," said Fart Weasel. Recalling the last time he got this angry, I shut up.

Mom forced me into the house. I wished I could escape back to Erin and Leigh's.

"Can I go to work?" I asked.

Fart Wesel snorted. "Like you have a real job."

"I do! And I'm scheduled tomorrow."

"No, you aren't. You probably just want to shoot up like your shithead brother."

"No, I have a job. . . ."

"Then where's the fucking money?" he said. "You owe us rent, you owe us for food. Just shut your mouth."

I shut it.

I hid in my room. I huddled next to my bed and tried to stop shaking. I texted Erin and gave her the brief rundown. She said she understood and that she and Leigh were there if I needed anything.

"I've been accused of harassing Adam. Have been captured by Mom and her husband. Am trapped," I texted to Michaela.

"What? Oh, Brynn. Can you get out?"

"Can't. Only allowed to leave for school."

"I'm so sorry, baby."

It helped a little that she called me baby. No one had ever done that before. But it was only like two seconds later that my mom barged in the room and demanded my phone. I deleted Michaela's whole text thread before she forced me to give it to her. I was too scared of Mom finding out about the whole gay thing on top of everything else that I didn't have energy left to miss all of Michaela's words.

All I could think to do was get out my laptop and write to you, Rachel. Mom tried to take that, too.

"Homework," I said.

"You get it for an hour each night."

The assholes changed the Wi-Fi password, so I couldn't even try to contact anyone that way.

I could hear her and Fart Weasel arguing about me. He wanted to throw me out so they could call the cops. She wanted to make him dinner. Finally she won. Later, after they were both asleep, I crept to the kitchen. There wasn't anything left in the refrigerator except ketchup.

It was a sad, ironic cafeteria reminder of what could bring a person to win or lose.

Sincerely,
Brynn

Folder: Inbox
To: Brynnieh0401@gmail.com
From: **Mail Delivery Subsystem** <mailer-daemon@googlemail.com>
Date: February 24
Subject: Dad

Delivery to the following recipient failed permanently

BarRodWireGuy62@gmail.com

Technical details of permanent failure:

Google tried to deliver your message, but it was rejected by the server for the recipient domain gmail.com

by gmail-smtp-in.l.google.com. [2a00:1490:400c:c0b::1b].

The error that the other server returned was:

550-5.1.1 The e-mail account that you tried to reach does not exist. Please try

550-5.1.1 double-checking the recipient's e-mail address for typos or

550-5.1.1 unnecessary spaces. Learn more at

550 5.1.1 https://support.google.com/mail/answer/6596 x67vy900421wma.125-gsmtp

—Original message—

Dear Dad,

This seems like it might be you. I did some deep web searching to find this.

Listen, Dad, I'm in trouble. Mom and the guy she married are awful. And I never did anything to you, did I? What did I ever do wrong that made you not want to talk to me?

I'm not like Nicholas, Dad. I never was. And even if I turned out exactly like him, shouldn't you love me anyway? Isn't that a dad's job?

Please just write and let me know if you are out there.

Sincerely,

Brynn

Folder: Sent
To: SteerlerRay62@smrrttmail.com
From: Brynnieh0401@gmail.com
Date: February 24
Subject: Please

Dear Dad,

It's Brynn. I have tried to contact you several other ways, but they have not worked.

Are you out there, Dad? Are you?

I don't suppose you'd want a cute, almost eighteen-year-old crashing on your couch for a few months, would you? You don't even need to feed me. I'll get a job. I'll pay rent.

Why don't you want me? Why does no one want me?

Your daughter,

Brynn

Folder: Drafts
To: Rachel@msnbc.com
From: Brynnieh0401@gmail.com
Date: February 25
Subject: Boom

Dear Rachel Maddow,

Heard on your podcast at the library (since there is no watching of the television now) that North Korea didn't detonate a hydrogen bomb even though they said they did. But they set off something, and that means that they are getting closer to the kind of bomb that can blow an island off the map. Super.

Speaking of things blowing up, or maybe just blowing, that is my life right now. Erin e-mailed that she and Leigh conspired to break me out of here, but then that would technically be kidnapping. Plus, I was late getting out from school today because Mr. Grimm kept me to give me a pep talk. Fart Weasel actually called the police and had them waiting for me when I got home. The officer must have been one of his buddies, because there is no way I could be considered a missing person if I was gone for an extra forty-five minutes. Learned that one from Nick's early days of using. Still, the officer put on a good show.

"You wouldn't like prison," he said. "You're too old for juvie. Women offenders would have a *good* time with you." He looked me up and down.

"Yes, sir," I said. Those were the only words that felt safe. I was only seventeen. I wasn't too old for juvie. *Thanks to the big bro for teaching me that, too.*

"Your daddy tells me you've been talking real big. Like you don't owe them anything, like you can make it on your own. Where you going to live, girl? Who is going to take care of you? You ain't seen anything. You have no idea. Next time I come by, you are coming with me to the station, you hear?"

"Yes, sir," I said. "May I go to my room to do homework?" I asked.

Fart Weasel snorted. "Homework. Sure." But he didn't care enough to argue.

I left before he could say anything else. I curled into a ball on Nick's old sleeping bag.

The fact is that I'm eighteen in less than a month. Three weeks and five days to be exact. My birthday falls on April 1. April Fools' Day! Appropriate because my life is a joke. When is your birthday, Rachel? I never thought to look it up. Maybe I'll send you a card.

I know the assholes that are keeping me here think they are proving something to me by exerting their legal authority. That I have no hope for a future without . . . what? Them? No. Fart Weasel barely finished high school himself, and even though Mom went to nursing school, it's not like she's frolicking through a meadow of hot dicks and dollar bills on the daily. Maybe they just want to prove that I have no hope for a future, period. And I am beginning to agree.

At least I could see Michaela at school. That was my one saving grace.

"When we are both eighteen, we'll get our own apartment," she said.

"We will eat pizza every night," I said.

"We can stay up as late as we want," she said.

"Doing *whatever* we want," I added.

She blushed. "Yes, please," she said.

But I admit that seemed so far away. How could I go to school and work enough to be on my own? And would Michaela really leave her gram?

I look at it like you would, Rachel. Look at the facts. Explain the story. Stay in it for the long sell, if you must, but compile the narrative with the available information and present the truth. So here it is: I can think. I can write the things I think. But they don't matter outside my head. That's why I type them to you and never send them. Because they aren't worth much. And even if I weren't shit at school, where would words get me? Definitely not Princeton or Penn or some place where People Who Will One Day Matter go. And there are even people better at selling underwear. So what is the point of trying? What is the point of anything?

The next to last time I saw Nick, he was coming down from a high.

He stumbled into the house, and Fart Weasel laid into him. Really let him have it. Didn't hit him, but unleashed a torrent of such unkindness that it scared me. Nick just laughed. Told him to fuck off. Fart Weasel just left the house mumbling about shitheads when it was over.

"How'd you do that?" I asked.

Nick shook his head. "When you realize nothing matters, Brynn, then you're truly free."

"Don't I at least matter to you?" I had asked.

"Oh, Brynnie" was all he said. He wrapped his arms around my head before he staggered outside and got in his car. I couldn't stop him.

At the time, I just chalked it up to his Zen and the Art of Fucking Up shtick, but now I see what he meant. When you realize that there is nothing left to care about, no one can hurt you.

There's my story, Rachel. Not so long a sell, really. Did I get any of that wrong? Did I miss anything? You always ask your expert guests that. Now I hand it back to you.

I hope North Korea doesn't bomb some place off the map. There are babies and dogs and daisies in places that all deserve to see the sun. That their lives could go up in a giant booming mushroom cloud sucks. But there's nothing I can do about it.

Sincerely,

Brynn

Folder:	Sent
To:	SteerlerRay62@smrrttmail.com
From:	Brynnieh0401@gmail.com
Date:	February 28
Subject:	Well, fuck you too

Dear Dad,

You could have written to me.

You didn't have to contact Mom. That was actually pretty shitty. You couldn't even ask her to hand her cell to me?

It made things worse. It's not like I even asked for money or anything.

Don't worry. I'll leave you alone from now on, asshole.

Brynn

Dear Rachel Maddow,

I looked it up. You and I have the same birthday. Seriously? I checked several sources. Would not have called that one. I think this pretty much disproves astrology 100 percent.

Sincerely,

Brynn

Folder: Drafts
To: Rachel@msnbc.com
From: Brynnieh0401@gmail.com
Date: March 3
Subject: Low

Dear Rachel Maddow,

Fart Weasel slapped me again. This time my mom wanted me to wash the dishes, and I said I would if I could have my phone back or at least go back to work.

"Do the fucking dishes," Fart Weasel said.

"Maybe we can negotiate," I said, my heart rising a little. "I could agree to do more around the house if—"

He got up and slapped me.

"Negotiate. Shut the fuck up. Do the dishes."

My face stung. I blinked back the tears the force of the strike had caused. I looked at Mom. The bags under her eyes looked darker than even yesterday. Her face pleaded with me.

"Just do them," she mouthed.

I couldn't even sigh. Breathing made the pain worse. I did the dishes.

It didn't leave a mark, so at least I didn't have to talk about it at school. I'd basically stopped speaking anyway. There just wasn't any point. Michaela tried daily to cheer me up, but I still felt numb.

"I'm sorry," was the only thing I could think to say to her.

"Please don't be sorry," she repeated. She looked as lost as I was.

The blue room tried to break the wall of numb.

"Brynn, have you seen Justin's stickers? He made them on his computer. Goth zombies! Hysterical! We are going to pass them out on the down low." That was Bianca.

"Brynn, you haven't turned in any work for last week yet. None. You were getting extra credit for the political campaign, but now that there isn't much to that . . ." That was Mr. Grimm.

"Are you okay? You don't look so good," Lacey said.

"Brynn, maybe your parents will let you come over to my place." That was Sarah. "They always liked me." I shrugged. But she was right. Mom gave me a two-hour reprieve to Sarah's house, mostly because I think she was sick of me being there.

I wanted to go to Michaela's. But I couldn't do that.

And anywhere was better than in Mom's house.

So I sat in Sarah's beanbag chair, idly leafing through a magazine. You were in it, Rachel.

"Did you know I have the same birthday as Rachel Maddow?" I said.

"No, I didn't. April Fools' Day, right? Funny." She smiled. She nudged me over and sat down next to me in the beanbag. It was not big enough for two people, and she kind of ended up in my lap.

"Is this okay?"

"I have a girlfriend."

"But she's not here," she said.

She smiled and started playing with my hair. In September, I would have killed for this. Maybe I would have only killed Adam or Fart Weasel, but still. Killed. Now I was smooth, my jagged edges rubbed off. There was only matte where once had been glossy, sea glass instead of a broken bottle. The idea of sea glass made me smile. Sarah thought it was because of her.

"Brynn, we should be together," Sarah said. "We made sense together."

"Why?" I asked. Her fingers drifted down to my shirt.

"Because."

"Because why?"

"Just because."

That wasn't an answer. I hated that. Even if my stupid life was shit, that still irked me. *Answer* the question. If you don't know the answer, fine. Say that. But don't act like you know and make the other person feel stupid for needing information to give themselves a chance.

Sarah shifted off of the beanbag until her chest stretched over my lap. She held herself up on either side of me, her lips brushing mine in a kiss.

"Come on, Brynn. I know things are tough. But let's just be together. This is easier, don't you think?" Her fingers traced a belt loop, then another, then the zipper of my jeans.

"Easier than what?"

"Good grief. I don't know. Not being together? Being with someone else? No offense, but it's not like you have many better options." Her voice softened. "We were great once."

I sank back into the chair and let her touch me. I didn't agree. We were never *great*. We were good. But only for a little while.

"What are you thinking?" she said.

"The campaigning sucked, and we're not allowed to do it anymore. But there's still time before the election for people to forget about me. Do you think Adam will win? If either of us is still allowed to be in it?" I asked.

She looked up and arched an eyebrow. "I don't know. He took a hit there. But . . . he has ways of getting out of things."

"I have no doubt."

"Those pictures . . ." She shifted her eyes nervously.

"Yeah?"

"It really wasn't you, right? Like, the underwear and the zombies weren't you, and neither were the pictures?"

I sat up. "No. Well, okay, the underwear was me, and the zombies were Justin. But not the pictures. I'd *never* do something like that. Lacey runs a clean campaign."

I wasn't going to ruin someone's life, even a slime mold ball sack someone's life, because of his or her bad choices. I knew what that could do to a person. I was no saint.

"Okay, okay. And they don't have *any* idea of who sent them, then?"

"No, they were from my account. So they think it's me. And there's no way to prove it wasn't me, I guess."

Sarah gave me a look I didn't understand.

Which was really weird, wasn't it? Shouldn't that upset her, if she wanted my name to be cleared?

"It. Wasn't. Me," I said. Anger wedged itself up from my stomach. It was almost refreshing to feel something other than a dull, formless suck.

"Okay, okay, it wasn't you."

She sounded like she believed that. No. Like she *knew*.

"I just thought you'd be happy to get the credit for that stunt. Or if you knew something, you would definitely tell me, right? Because we might be together, or something, and if you knew something bad, you could tell me." She looked nervous again.

"Sarah, what are you even talking about? You know what? You were right last summer. I *am* too much drama. And if you think I'd approve of shit like that . . . then you don't know me. Maybe you never really knew me at all. Because Rachel Maddow would think that was sketchy. Well, okay, maybe she'd put it on the air after the info was vetted and shit. But she wouldn't pull some sort of *Adamesque* anonymous crap. And if Rachel wouldn't do that, then I wouldn't do that."

"Oh please. Like you even still watch her. You just liked her because I did. If you don't know what I'm talking about with the pictures, or who else would have them, then never mind."

I shook my head. "Bye, Sarah," I said. I got up and walked out of her room and out of her house. She didn't stop me.

She was right, in a way. I don't still watch you, since I can't. That sunk in. You were basically the one constant I had left.

Sincerely,
Brynn

Folder: Drafts
To: Rachel@msnbc.com
From: Brynnieh0401@gmail.com
Date: March 7
Subject: Countdown

Dear Rachel Maddow,

I am very, very close to eighteen. At eighteen, I can move out and quit school, and there isn't a thing Mom and Fart Weasel can do. I can hide at Erin and Leigh's for a week or two. That's all it will take for them to lose interest in me.

Since I can't text, I thought about writing e-mails to everyone I knew. Though, the only contacts I have in this e-mail are Mr. Grimm, Lacey, Erin, Michaela, and you, since I technically opened this account just for you.

I should really try to meet some more people.

Today I loathed life in my silent stupor when we were sent to the cafeteria for lunch. Lance had some sort of assessments, and they wanted his familiar room. I gathered my bleak tray and noticed a slop of gray peas forming tributaries of pea juice along a mount of mashed potatoes. I sat down next to Michaela, who put her arm around me. It's all she could think to do these days. I gave her a small smile.

"Hello, crew," said Justin, looming over me. "Welcome to the fray."

"They made us come up here with yinz randos." Bianca laughed.

"We did not come willingly," said Lacey, but her face evidenced she was totally in love with Justin, too.

I said nothing, just watched the peas drip, drip, drip.

"Yo, Brynn," said Justin. "You okay there, or are you having a moment with your food?"

Still I said nothing. Riley nudged Bianca.

"She's in a bad place since the *accusation*."

"Why?" Justin frowned.

"You know. She was accused of sabotaging Adam."

"I thought you were cleared of that," Justin said to me.

"Not to my knowledge, no," I said. "He is under investigation for the War Memorial thing. I am under investigation for alerting everyone to the War Memorial thing. It's awesome."

"Everyone thinks Brynn did it," said Bianca.

I glared at her.

"But they are happy you did!" she added.

I shrugged.

Justin continued to frown the whole time he sat with us.

He caught up with me later as I was kissing Michaela good-bye before she got on her school bus.

"Brynn. Dude. Stop. You're kind of scaring me."

"Why?" I asked.

"Uh, you aren't speaking? You even kind of ignored Michaela and Lacey. You look as pale as one of the zombies half the student body actually thinks you have killed. Like, legit, they think you kill zombies. Who are these people?" He rolled his eyes.

I shrugged again.

"See? You didn't even smile. Brynn. Seriously, talk to me," he said.

I looked at him. He stared back at me, his wide eyes the color of his freckles. I never noticed that before.

"You answered my question," I said.

"What question?"

"Why you were worried. You actually had an answer. With examples. That's refreshing."

So unlike, say, Adam. I hope Justin wins treasurer, even if he has to work with uncontested Sarah (which was likely, as he was still unopposed as well).

Justin looked bewildered. "Right. Okay. Where are you going?"

"Home."

"Where's that?"

I shrugged. If I thought about it, nowhere really.

"Can I walk you?"

"My stepfather will think you are banging me for money."

"Shut up."

When I didn't smile, he whistled. "I'll take the risk."

We walked in silence for at least a quarter mile. "Brynn," he said finally, "is there anything I can do? You're cool. But you aren't you these days. It's like you're . . . broken somehow."

All I could do was grimace. We walked in silence for a while again and reached my crappy street.

"This is my stop," I said. "You know, there is something you can do for me."

"What? Anything."

"Win the election for me."

"That I can't do, Madam Candidate."

I didn't say anything.

"Promise me you'll vote in a couple of weeks, Brynn. For yourself. Every single one counts, you know. *'Now more than ever the people are responsible for the character of their Congress. If that body be ignorant, reckless, and corrupt, it is because the people tolerate ignorance, reckless-ness, and corruption.'* James Garfield said that."

"Okay, I'll vote," I said.

"Promise me."

"I promise."

"Good. I'll see you later." He waved.

That was a good quote. Stupid James Garfield and his fucking com-pelling arguments. Because heaven forbid Adam won by one fucking vote.

Sincerely,

Brynn

Folder:	Spam
To:	Brynnieh0401@gmail.com
From:	michaelagjordan@westing.pa.edu
Date:	March 9
Subject:	Countdown

Hey, baby,

You know I'm not much of an e-mailer. You seem so down lately. I'm sorry I'm not much help. If there's anything I can ever do, please let me know. I'm here for you. Well, I'm not *here* here—I'm at my grandmother's. But I meant what I said. We could move in together.

Love,

M

Folder: Drafts
To: Rachel@msnbc.com
From: Brynnieh0401@gmail.com
Date: March 12
Subject: One Week Out

Dear Rachel Maddow,

The student body votes for its elected officials in a week. Not since . . . the last national election . . . have there been candidates with such sketchy rumors going around about them.

That sentence should be more dramatic. The time of questionable public servants should be past us. But maybe nothing is ever in the past. This kind of stuff sleeps until someone pokes it and wakes it up and it takes a dump on everyone around it.

There. That had impact, as Mr. Grimm would say. Maybe I should try to be a speechwriter.

Justin informed me that Adam still thinks I sent out the pictures of him, and that Adam is out for blood. Which is reasonable, since the pictures that could get him in a shitload of trouble came from my account.

"Are you sure you didn't send them?" asked Justin.

"Actually, there was a day or two I don't remember recently. Who knows what went down then."

"Seriously?"

"No, Justin. God." I sighed. "I had no pictures with which to blackmail Adam. And if I did, I would have told Lacey, and she would have tried to talk me out of using them."

"Damn right I would," said Lacey.

"And then I would have probably sent them anyway because my heart is a small, dead thing. But Lacey would have rolled her ass to Maynard's faster than you can say 'dirty politics.' And even *that* wouldn't have mattered, because I would have probably accidently carbon-copied Rachel Maddow and you and Mr. Grimm for good measure."

Justin considered this for a second. "Yeah," he finally agreed. "It's a shame. You were pretty epic in the debate."

"No, I wasn't."

"Yes. Yes, you were. Your girl Michaela helped you out, but you had it together. You touched me." Justin put his hand to his heart.

"And look at me now. The subject of controversy," I said.

"All publicity is good publicity," said Lacey.

"Do you actually believe that?" I narrowed my eyes at her.

She kind of shrugged. "You didn't send the pictures. You stood up to Adam in public. You were *articulate*. You had my vote, Brynn. But now it's because you've really earned it."

Rachel, honestly, what matters more than that? Lacey thinks I'm articulate. Adam can take his accusations and shove them up his ballot box. Even if Justin seemed worried about retaliation from Adam, what more could Adam do to me? He already went after Nick. He couldn't possibly sink lower than that.

Mr. Maynard e-mailed the school tech guys, but they don't seem to have the time to clear my name, since they cover several districts. I still wondered who the fuck could even do that. Adam wasn't stupid enough to frame himself. His buddies weren't smart enough to frame him. Who else was left? Sarah?

Actually.

The only person who might know my password (which until a few weeks ago was ChrisHayesRulz!) was also Sarah.

But how would she . . .

There were rumors of pictures. I heard about them from Justin, but Sarah was in journalism, too. Maybe she got them from one of the Honors kids who had been with Adam. Maybe she had been there, too?

That was crazy. There was no way. Why would she take me out, too? This was before I gave her the big brush-off.

I have to go to bed. I go a little too conspiracy theory in the head if I stay up too late.

Sincerely,

Brynn

Folder: Drafts
To: Rachel@msnbc.com
From: Brynnieh0401@gmail.com
Date: March 13
Subject: Shoe leather reporting

Dear Rachel Maddow,

The question about Sarah stayed in my brain. If I thought about it for any length of time, the answer was simple. It had to be her.

Sarah didn't actually want to be student body vice president. I knew this about her. I'd bet a lot of money she only ran for that position because Adam wanted to be in charge, and there was no way anyone in their little cult would take him on.

What Sarah *really* wanted was to be student body president. To do that, she'd have to get rid of Adam. If she had those pictures, all she had to do was sit on them until the right time.

But then I entered the race. So then she had to get rid of Adam *and* me.

Did Sarah ever want to get back together with me? If she had, I bet she had thought that she could live with being vice president, because she could just tell me what to do if I got elected.

Then she must have changed her mind. Instead, she decided to screw me over, too. Maybe she just wanted all the attention and power for herself. Sharing it with me was too much for her to take.

And she assumed I'd never suspect her. Because she knew good ol' Brynnie still had feelings for her.

Fuck me. She was right about that. At least for a while.

But she made a mistake using my school e-mail. Because I knew she was the only one who knew my password. It'd been the same since ninth grade.

I made Michaela wait for Justin with me outside of the journalism room. "Justin," I said when I saw him. "How good are you with comput-ers?" I asked.

"Okay. Not my geek fu, if you know what I mean," he said.

"I don't. But you are likely better than me. So, you know how I have been unjustly accused?"

"Yes."

"I think I know who might have had my password. But I can't prove it. Is there a way to see when someone got in my e-mail?"

Michaela grimaced. I told her that I thought Sarah might be behind this whole thing, and she was ready to shove her in a locker and throw away the key.

"Well, the e-mail itself would have a time and date stamp on it," he said.

"Yeah, but is there another way? Like, could you tell *where* someone was logging on to my e-mail?"

Justin thought. "Yes. Maybe. The Westing High e-mail has you put in an alternate address. It makes you update it every year. Did you ever do that?"

I frowned. I had put this, my Rachel account, in at some point, but there is never anything in the inbox of this one.

"Yeah, I have an e-mail from an assignment I used this year. But Greg and Lance showed me how to just filter all that stuff into another folder."

"Well, if someone logged in from a funky location, your school e-mail might have sent you a notice."

A light bulb flickered dimly over my head. It's like I could look up and see it, like you would in a cartoon.

"Maybe there's something in there?" Michaela said.

Justin's eyes lit up. Even if it was because I was in a deep pile of shit, at the moment we were political investigative journalists.

"Maybe," he breathed.

I tore my laptop out of my backpack and logged on. And do you know what was in that filter folder?

A notice. From my school account. I had logged on from an unfamiliar location twice. But it wasn't me. They were sent from the school library, if I understood what the e-mail was telling me. And I hadn't used the school library computers in ages.

"I would guess the cameras in the library work. *Because* of all those computers the school just got. Maybe whoever framed you used machines at school to make it look like you did it," said Michaela. You could practically hear venom in her voice.

I threw her a grateful smile. "Thanks for having my back."

"Let's go see Maynard," said Justin.

The computer might have saved me. Who would have thought that?

Sincerely,

Brynn

Folder: Drafts
To: Rachel@msnbc.com
From: Brynnieh0401@gmail.com
Date: March 14
Subject: How low can you go?

Dear Rachel Maddow,

Debunktion junction, what's my function? Toot, toot! In an earlier corre-spondence I believe I said that Adam couldn't sink any lower. Is that true or false? False, Rachel! Toot, toot!

Because going after me was mean, but pretty stupid. Going after my dead brother was asshattery. Far as I can tell, the dead don't give a shit what sort of posters go up about them. But today. Well, yesterday went to a whole new level. And wouldn't you know, it all went down right after I told Mr. Maynard that I might have proof that I was innocent after all.

After we went to Maynard's office, the bell that ended Justin and Michaela's study hall rang, so they had to go back to class. It was in the blue room that everything went wrong.

"Um, Brynn?" Bianca whispered. Ms. Yee had started teaching. "There's something you need to see," she said.

"What?" I whispered.

"Lunch," she said.

So at lunch, Lacey, Riley, Bianca, Greg, and Lance formed a semicir-cle around Bianca's phone. They seemed to already know what she was going to show me.

"This isn't necessary," said Lacey. "She doesn't need to see it."

Bianca shook her head at Lacey. "Yeah, she does." Bianca looked at me. "We got this, today. On Insta," she said. "But I think it's been sent out other places, too. I texted a couple of people to check. Um. Most people have seen it, you know. Small school."

"Is this about my brother?" I asked.

"No," said Bianca. She showed me the video.

"Students of Westing," said a deep voice. "All of you have secrets. Some of them bad. Some of them worse. Some of them downright terrifying." Horror music played.

My stomach dropped. Jesus S. Christ, what was left to say about me?

"A new student came to Westing a few months ago, and no one took notice. Why would we? She was hidden from view. But you can't hide what you do in the dark. Because someone will eventually shine a light on you." Familiar images flashed. Oh, holy sweet asshole slime ball sacks. There were bare legs. And toned, flat abs. I squinted, unable to look away. Man, Adam really knew how to get back at a person. That shattered me, for a second.

But Rachel.

It certainly wasn't me.

Or Nick.

Or Sarah.

It was Michaela.

Michaela surrounded by people, clearly not sober. Or awake. Wearing very little. Michaela. Exposed.

"Tsk, tsk. Bad girls like bad girls."

That stopped me. In spite of everything. "Oh my God. Are you serious? All those people standing around at that party or whatever it is? That's exploitation, you shit-eating son of fucking Satan," I screamed at Bianca's phone.

"Everything okay over there?" said Mr. Grimm.

Some picture of Michaela stayed on the screen at the end of the video, but I couldn't stand to look at it.

At the end of the video, I put my head in my hands. I tried texting her from Bianca's phone. It was all over the whole school by dismissal for sure.

All of this way my fault. My fucking fault. For what? For giving a damn? Is this how it is, Rachel? I've looked you up online before. The things people say about you. Such terrible, terrible things. You went to Stanford, you got yourself a Rhodes Scholarship, you earned a kick-ass job on TV. But people skewer you like a woman-kabob because you show what you know (and they don't). At the end of the day, it just goes to show that even the best of us are punching bags for the mean and stupid. And those who aren't the best? Well. We're just trash, aren't we?

Fuck it, Rachel. Fuck it all. I'm done.

Sincerely,
Brynn

Folder: Inbox
To: Brynnieh0401@gmail.com
From: Egrimm@westing.pa.edu
Date: March 15
Subject: RE: The Ides

Dear Rachel Maddow,

I didn't forget the questions I am supposed to answer for you. I didn't answer the last two from Mr. Grimm. I am answering them now to stop him from staring at me like I'm about to explode from patheticness. [You have many admirable qualities, Brynn. Chief among them is that you keep at things. Even if they take several months and are technically way overdue, you still stick with them. I admire that.] I avoided the last one—"What could you do to change what bothers you?" And I just skipped the last one, "What inspires you?" altogether. I figured since I obviously wasn't going to send any of these to you, why bother? But I was struck when I came back to school today. Same old hallways, same smartphones everywhere that replayed Michaela's video over and over, same blue room. Greg, Lance, Riley, and Bianca could barely look at me. But Lacey came right over to me.

"Are you still running?" she asked.

I sucked in my breath to say no. I wasn't running. I was doing as little as possible until I turned eighteen in a little more than two weeks, and then I was dropping out and working a million hours in retail for the rest of my life. Anything was better than this shit. But I looked at Lacey. I know she'd be pissed off if I told her she inspired me. But that was the truth. She inspires the fuck out of me. Not because she overcame adversity and shit, but because she's always stuck by me. She's smart and kind and awesome amidst a universe filled with ~~twats~~ dickwad scrotum pubes. [Brynn. You do remember I'm a teacher, yes?] And even if she could find a more interesting person to try to help out, she picked me.

In that moment, when I was there looking at her, her being my one true friend left at this stupid school . . . I couldn't do it. I *wouldn't* quit. I remember what it felt like when I thought Nick could get his shit together but didn't. I had a choice here. Goddamnit I'm going to grab agency by the nads and use that motherfucker to try to enact change. [Have you considered asking Lacey or another classmate to read your assignments before you turn them in? I know she used to give you feedback. . . .]

"Yeah. I'm still running for the stupid SGA president. I mean, people vote in days. Might as well."

"Yeeeahhhhh!" Lacey said.

I grinned in spite of myself.

"Is Michaela okay?" Lacey asked.

My grin faded. "I don't know," I said. "I haven't talked to her since yesterday. I tried to call. And text her from Justin's phone. A bunch. I haven't seen her around at school. Have you?" I asked hopefully.

"Oh," Lacey said. "No. I'm sorry." We stared at each other for a painful moment.

"Though, you know, Ms. Willis," I said slowly. "This makes me a person with pretty much nothing left to lose."

"Okay . . ." Lacey said slowly.

"Yup. Aren't people like that . . . dangerous?"

"Yes . . ."

"So I might as well see if I win this thing, right?"

"Yes, Brynn. One hundred percent."

What can I say? I'm at the end of my rope. And when I'm at the end of my rope? I take no prisoners.

[Again, here you are, so persistent. In the midst of defeat, turmoil. Here you are acting on *your* beliefs, instead of just remaining inactive. Brava, Brynn!]

Sincerely,
Brynn

Folder: Drafts
To: Rachel@msnbc.com
From: Brynnieh0401@gmail.com
Date: March 19
Subject: Election Day

Dear Rachel Maddow,

Got my grades today. I got all As. Maybe Mr. Grimm and Ms. Yee gave them out of pity or guilt or confusion. Maybe I got partial credit for writing to you and not cowering before Adam. I could be on the paper again, if I weren't likely dropping out next month.

SGA set up an official polling place in the gym. There were tables with little cardboard dividers. You had to check in to receive your ballot. Mr. Maynard had taken great pains to tell everyone three times a day all of March to bring the school ID. I voted for Justin and myself and the other uncontested offices. I wrote in Lawrence O' Donnell's name as a protest vote for the VP position instead of Sarah. Someone should really do pep rallies to get people more interested in down-ticket races. And running for them. When public service is as important as football or wrestling at Westing High, then maybe we'd be getting somewhere.

I folded my form and shoved it into the wooden ballot box, manned by Sarah. We avoided each other's eyes as I turned away. I sat silently in the blue room for the rest of the day. Voting ended at 2:00, so the results would be announced at the end of school. The blue room clock doesn't tick. The second hand whirs around silently. I watched it for far too many seconds. Five minutes before the final bell, the intercom crackled to life.

"Good afternoon, students," said Mr. Maynard. "I have your SGA election results." The blue room hushed. Lacey rolled over to me. I tried to give her a small smile, but it was too exhausting.

"Secretary, Phillip Brenner. Treasurer, Justin Mitchell. Vice president, Sarah Livingston. And the SGA president for next year is . . ." He paused. "Adam Graff."

An audible groan went up in the blue room. And the red room and yellow room and green room. My brain grew comfortably numb. If before the numbness had ebbed and flowed, now it took up permanent residence. No anger, or sadness, or loss, or anything flitted through.

"I'm sorry, Brynn," said Lacey. "At least we tried, right?"

My head nodded at her. "Yup. At least we tried."

And failed, Rachel. Again.

Sincerely,

Brynn

Folder:	Sent
To:	Brynnieh0401@gmail.com
From:	Egrimm@westing.pa.edu
Date:	March 22
Subject:	RE: School Assignment

Dear Brynn,

As you are likely aware, I taught your brother my first and his last year here at Westing High. I can honestly say that of anyone I've ever met, your brother was the best kind of person: hardworking, nice to people, full of original ideas. Did you know that he convinced several of us to have a carnival in the parking to raise money for cancer research, because another student in his class had leukemia? He was the best.

I know you miss him. *I* miss him, and he was only my student for one year. I see so much of him in you. And you might think that means you are doomed. But was he doomed when he was a kid trying to help his friend? Was he doomed when he had a straight-A report card? I don't think he was. I don't think he was doomed until the second he OD'd.

Every second before that he had a chance. You are like him before his choices and before the illness of opiates took him. You have a chance in every second of every day. You'll make mistakes, because that's what people do. But you can make it. Nick would be so, so thrilled with the person you have become.

Your assignments this year have been as inspiring as they were scatological in content. That is saying something, young lady. Don't give up. There will be countless chances out there to do good in the world.

Warmly,

Mr. Grimm

Folder:	Sent
To:	mmaynard@westing.pa.edu
From:	wbird@westing.pa.edu
Date:	March 25
Subject:	

Dear Mark,

"I've been the janitor here through six principals. We've had those cameras for three. You're the first who made me do something with them. Here are them recordings you wanted."

—Bill

P.S. Hi, Mr. Maynard! It's Will, Bill's son. I hope you're doing well. Dad had me type this for him. I came in and found the video footage of the library you wanted. Attached you will find the digital files. I hear this might be because of some controversy over the school elections? How some things never change at ol' Westing. Thanks!

Folder: Sent
To: mmaynard@westing.pa.edu
From: JSG@GraffHunterWexley.net
Date: March 26
Subject: Investigation

Dear Principal Maynard,

As you may have been aware, the investigation surrounding the War Memorial has been concluded. I will not apologize for Adam's behavior. He has been targeted for years at Westing High and finally broke due to all the stress.

His cooperation in the investigation has been beyond reproach. It is unacceptable that you should now suspend him and not the other students (the ones not so clearly visible in the alleged pictures). Much to my chagrin, we will be pulling him from continuing at Westing High. It is clear that he will be unable to receive unbiased instruction at your school, despite the fact that he would have been the elected leader of his peers.

Also, here is a list of students present the night of the War Memorial incident who should also be punished, the way my son has been.

Sincerely,

Jonathan S. Graff, Esquire

Students in
incident.docx
21 KB

W

Folder:	Sent
To:	GloriaMaynard@smrrttmail.com
From:	mmaynard@westing.pa.edu
Date:	March 27
Subject:	Summer vacation . . . permanently

Dear Glory,

Honey, honest to God, these kids are going to kill me. After all of the political intrigue and crappola I ranted about this week, I *still* don't think that student I keep talking about is going to end up on Student Government. The kid who set fire to the War Memorial is still disqualified. That's great, his dad is such a giant pain. And *then* we found out the girl who won the vice president spot broke into her ex-girlfriend's e-mail and sent all of those incriminating photos of the first kid. (Her *ex-girlfriend, who was the other student running for president.* Are you following this? It's like one of your damn shows. . . .) So then the vice president girl was disqualified. But the bylaws won't allow a candidate who didn't win to hold the office if there are other people who can be bumped up. She could run for secretary, maybe.

It's a shame. The whole school would have benefited from having her. I don't even know if I can explain this whole thing to her because of privacy concerns. I'm going to ask the superintendent.

Tonight I say we open a bottle (or two) of wine and seriously look into downsizing. You were right—life is short. We don't need the huge house and neither one of us actually *likes* traveling. I could retire this year. I know you love your job, so we could survive pretty well off your efforts (like you've suggested since I moved into administration).

Also, Cynthia is going to have that baby any day now, and she is not going to turn down free childcare from a grandpa with three master's degrees in education.

Love,

Mark

Folder:	Sent
To:	STUDENTS; PARENTS
Cc:	TRUSTEES
From:	mmaynard@westing.pa.edu
Date:	March 28
Subject:	SGA Election Results

Dear Westing High Community,

Due to events that have come to light the past week, the results of the recent Student Government presidential election are considered void. According to Article IV of the SGA charter:

"Should a student be unwilling or unable to perform the duties assigned to a Student Body President, or should he or she be found in violation of the Westing High Honor Code, the Vice President will assume the rights and duties of the position. The Vice President will have the power to appoint his or her successor. Should the Vice President be unwilling or ineligible, the Secretary may fulfill the role, or the Treasurer. Offices below that of President may be fulfilled by appointment or by a new electoral process."

As such, it is my pleasure to announce that the student body treasurer-elect, Justin Mitchell, will be the new Westing High student body president.

Please join me in congratulating Justin, and feel free to e-mail any questions or concerns you may have concerning this matter.

Sincerely,

Mark M. Maynard

Folder: Drafts
To: Rachel@msnbc.com
From: Brynnieh0401@gmail.com
Date: March 29
Subject: The opposite

Dear Rachel Maddow,

If there is joy in the suffering of others, is there suffering in the joy of others? There must be. And there must be a German word for it.

Man, did the shit ever hit the fan after the election. I don't know what happened to Sarah. But even though Adam is in a ball sack load of trouble, he is still coming out ahead. He is transferring to a fancy boarding school near the city. Apparently his dad has connections.

This didn't bother me. Much. You know I would lose my mind without the blue room to keep me sane, so I wasn't going anywhere near Adam's new digs. Justin would be in charge next year, too, and I had high hopes that he would undo Adam's legacy of suck. I was one weekend away from the legal freedom to sell underwear and live in a tent next to Erin and Leigh's trailer if I had to. It was all good. I had done my part to try to keep Adam from taking his first step toward running the world. The sisterhood may not have prevailed, but the failure wasn't as epic as I first thought.

I still didn't know who sent those e-mails about him. Mr. Maynard said he was still looking into it. And Sarah was disqualified from her office for some reason. Rumor had it that she was with Adam and the other kids who set the War Memorial on fire, but I doubted that. I couldn't ask her. Hopefully Justin and the intrepid staff of the *Westing High Gazette* could break that story.

I basked in this schadenfreude so much it kept me from paying attention as I was crossing the street in front of the school. A shiny blue hybrid nearly mowed me down.

"Whoa, watch it, asshole," I said, reeling back on my tiptoes before I stepped off the curb.

"I'd be careful if I were you," said Adam from the driver's seat.

"Oh, you. It's always you. Why can't you just drive into a ditch?" I stepped away from him. "Or better yet, get expelled or flunk at your new school, or go to jail or something."

Adam laughed. "No, I'll leave that to you, thanks."

"Do the world a favor and explode. Thanks."

"Oh, Brynn, I'll miss our witty repartee, really. Maybe one day we'll meet again."

"Only if Space hell is real," I muttered.

"What?"

"Nothing. Don't you have to go ruin someone else's day? Leave me alone."

"I don't ruin things. I just take care of what I need to. I'm still going to go to Princeton. Will actually be better prepared, since I'll be going to the sweet boarding school my mom's brothers went to. This whole thing finally made the old pops cough up the dough to send me. I'm going to be just fine. You'll still be in trouble for sending that shit out about me, even if I don't really think you were smart enough to do it. I think you were played, too, and you don't even know. *That's* actually the best part of this." He laughed. A real, genuine, "I think this is funny" laugh. At my life.

With that, he put his car in gear and drove off. A bit of oily water splashed on my jeans.

I thought about that while on the walk home. While I sat next to my bed, staring at the wall. While eating the burned steak Mom threw in front of me. While staring at the ceiling from Nick's sleeping bag as I failed to sleep. Adam was right. Maybe someone else had "won" this time, but that didn't mean Adam had lost. He still had everything now, and everything in front of him. The crushing weight of inevitable reality forced itself onto my rib cage. My lungs tried to rise but couldn't. All I could try to choke in was failure and disappointment and chances lost.

So often politics and power trump compassion and reason, right? Even you can't deny that. Why can't Congress pass anything? Why do even the most horrible candidates rise to the top of the heap in real-world elections?

Because the Adam Graffs of the world win in the end.

The Brynns . . . not so much.

So what's the point of trying? Honestly, what?

Sincerely,
Brynn

Folder: Drafts
To: Rachel@msnbc.com
From: Brynnieh0401@gmail.com
Date: April 1
Subject: April Fools'

Dear Rachel Maddow,
Happy birthday.

Sincerely,
Brynn

Dear Rachel Maddow,

Yesterday I left. I had nothing to pack, nothing but the clothes on my back, and my backpack with my laptop, really. I had brought it home because I didn't intend to go back to school. Mom and Fart Weasel didn't even look up when I came into the room. If Mom remembered it was my birthday, she didn't let on. I went over to Leigh and Erin's. I still had a key to their place. I let myself in and no one was home. I went to the room I stayed in and noticed that it seemed distinctly occupied by someone else. The bed was messy, and there were clothes strewn around the floor. The stuff that I had left there was neatly packed away in two boxes in the closet labeled "Brynn." My heart sank. I couldn't expect them to wait for me. I couldn't expect anything, from anyone. I hadn't done anyone any favors in this life. Space God had moved on, hopefully to the hopes and dreams of starving children or something. A couple of bras on the floor caught my eye. Deep plum. Oh, Aerie. I actually kind of missed it there. Erin must be running some sort of halfway house for wayward stock people. I sat down on the bed. I ran my fingers on the soft quilt. I lay down, tired. So tired. Of life and guys like Adam and of being too much and not enough all at once. Just like Nick.

I stayed there for what felt like hours. I slept part of the time. Once, I got up to go to the bathroom and steal food from the refrigerator. Eventually it got dark. Maybe they were off to Europe together. They joined a circus troupe or started a band. Or maybe everyone was just at work. I didn't know. I looked out the window into the dim street. Out there were more Adam Graffs and more Nick Harpers. The Graffs were lucky. They had cars and houses and careers and nice things. And power. All the power.

The Nicks wanted to be that other guy, but they were stuck in dead-end jobs and punches for marriages and shit. I was a Nick. I always would be.

I realized something then. If I was a Nick, I should really be a Nick. His supplier probably still squats at this abandoned warehouse down by the Monongahela.

So, that's where I'm going. Nick always repeated something about living in a van down by the river. I could try that. Maybe,

Maybe.

Maybe?

if only . . .

why not?

because.

Rachel, I want to thank you. I appreciate you keeping me company and telling me about the world all these years.

It occurs to me now that I'm back here, I could watch your show. They have fucking satellite now, and their DVR shit has been recording you. It looks like they've forgotten to get rid of them for weeks. Maybe I will watch. Once more, for old times' sake.

I look at all of these e-mails I've written to you. There are probably at least a hundred pages of them here. For what? Nothing useful. Nothing good. Just words alone with no one to read them. I'll finish this last letter and then delete it with the rest of them. They are easy enough to get rid of. Like a person. Like a life. Like Nick and me and everybody like us. A few stupid moves, and we all go away.

But not Adam. No.

Eventually he will win.

Love,
Brynn

Dear Brynn,

I am not sure what you sent me. I thought it was your school assignment from way back in the fall, but it looks like your journal?

I'm sorry I read some. I didn't understand what was going on. I scrolled to the end when I figured out what you had done. Did you mean to send this? Write me back, please. I had no idea how you were feeling. Let me know if you are okay or if there's anything I can do. Please don't do anything to hurt yourself, Brynn. A lot of people would miss you.

Love,

Lacey

Folder: Inbox
To: Brynnieh0401@gmail.com
From: Egrimm@westing.pa.edu
Date: April 2
Subject: RE: Finished

Dear Brynn,

Where are you right now? I don't know if you meant to send this to me or not, but I am actively worried about you. Please get back to me as soon as possible. Call my cell: 570-555-0198.

Thanks,

Evan Grimm

Folder:	Spam
To:	Brynnieh0401@gmail.com
From:	michaelagjordan@westing.pa.edu
Date:	April 2
Subject:	(no subject)

Brynn?!

Jesus Christ, are you still at home? Or somewhere else? Is your phone still off?

I can't leave Gram alone. Let me see if my uncle can get off work early. Please just be okay.

Folder:	Sent
To:	Rachel@msnbc.com
From:	Brynnieh0401@gmail.com
Date:	April 4
Subject:	Please disregard

!This message was sent with high importance !

Dear Rachel Maddow,

You may have received numerous e-mails from me recently. They were an extension of a school project I never meant to send. Please disregard them. I'm sorry I basically spammed you with my life story.

Sincerely,
Brynn Harper

Folder:	Drafts
To:	Brynnieh0401@gmail.com
From:	Brynnieh0401@gmail.com
Date:	April 7
Subject:	Inpatient

Dear Rachel Maddow,

I have learned several valuable life lessons over the past few days. I think the most important one was that you should keep a journal offline, not in your e-mail drafts folder. Because if you choose to put every thought in your head in an e-mail, and then save that e-mail to a folder, and then try to delete that folder, it is possible to accidentally send the entire thing to everyone you know. You will then have to live knowing that you did that.

Whoops.

I also learned that, upon finding several six-packs in a friend's refrigerator, a girl should not down it all out of self-loathing and despair. Actually, no one should ever drink that much for any reason, as even doing it out of sheer joy can lead to potential alcohol poisoning.

After I thought I deleted all my stupid e-mails (something I failed to do even stone-cold sober), I tuned in to you. But being alone with only my own head, even with you there, drove me bonkers. That's when I went fishing in the fridge. I've never been a big drinker, and frankly Leigh apparently favors beer fermented with cigarette smoke chased by ass. But I drank it all anyway. I quit tasting anything after three or four beers.

You prefer fancy mixed cocktails. Are they better? Because holy fucks that beer was *awful*.

Anyway, I didn't know my stomach could fit that much liquid, but after a few, I was thirstier and thirstier to escape my own head, so I just kept downing them. Your voice softened, the lights softened, the pounding in my chest slowed to near oblivion. It wasn't that I wanted to die. Just wanted to feel something other than loss for a change.

Erin beat the police I guess Michaela called by a few minutes, I'm told. Like four ambulances showed up for Brynnie "Never a Dull Moment" Harper. I earned myself an ambulance to the ER for nearly choking on my own puke.

The next thing I remember was gagging on a tube in my throat. That's what they do now; that whole "getting your stomach pumped," isn't technically true anymore. Mom was there. I wasn't dead. Thanks, Space God.

The moment my eyes cleared, the first thing I saw was Mom's look of sad disgust that before this point had been reserved especially for Nick. But now I was the new Nick.

"You forgot my birthday," I croaked after they removed my tube.

"That's why you did this?" she asked.

"No," I said.

"Then why?"

I didn't have an easy answer for that. "Because life sucks," I said.

A nurse who had just walked into my pod overheard that. She turned and walked right back out. Mom shook her head. Her scrubs were the same pale pink as her skin.

"Am I at your hospital?" I asked.

"Yes."

"They didn't bring me here on purpose," I said, meaning Erin and probably Leigh. Mom turned and looked at the wall. I noticed a blurry person-shape in the direction of her gaze.

"I know."

"Is that why he isn't here?" We both knew who I meant. The person-shaped smudge over by the wall neither reeked nor yelled, so I knew it couldn't be that Guy Mom Chose Over Me. The smudge had more of an Erin-like form.

"I didn't tell him you were here. I just said I was called in to cover someone's shift."

"Are you going to tell him?"

"You are still on my insurance. And this is my hospital. So I'll straighten out the bill without him. Shouldn't be too bad." She sounded almost proud about that.

"Okay."

"But then we're done." Her game face shifted back into place. "You're on your own now, Brynn."

She seemed to think this was new information to me.

"Yeah."

Mom got up and left. The blurred shape moved to me. Before Erin could speak, the nurse from before came back with two doctors.

"Sweetheart, we're here to ask some questions," she said.

"Do you know how much you drank?"

"Your blood work came back okay, but did you take anything? Did you plan to take anything?"

"Do you have any further plans to harm yourself?"

"How . . ."

"Why . . ."

"When . . ."

"How much . . ."

"Will you . . ."

Truth be told, Rachel, I don't know if this is how it went down. I don't remember much. Overwashed sheets scratched my legs. My feet couldn't get warm, even when Erin sat on them. My throat hurt, my eyes burned, Mom gave up for good. White coats purred sympathetically with invasive questions. I reconstruct it now for your sake.

That's not the truth, either. Technically I'm reconstructing it for the shrink. Erin brought my laptop so I can "journal my feelings." I tried to journal but found it impossible to write a word if it wasn't to you.

"That's weird," said Erin as she watched me talk to my computer on day two of my inpatient stay in the unlocked psych unit.

"Which part?"

"That you can't talk about your feelings unless you are pouring them out to Rachel Maddow."

"You don't know her. She's very easy to talk to."

"You have never met her," Erin said.

"I have spent hundreds of hours with her. I've seen her talk to other people. How different is it really?" I yawned and shifted in the spectacularly uncomfortable bed. Erin sighed.

"You scared the shit out of us," she said.

"I'm sorry. I didn't mean to."

"I know," she said. "I'm the one who should be sorry."

"What?" I asked.

"I thought maybe you needed some space to figure things out after you had to quit Aerie. But when you never texted or anything after that, I realized I shouldn't have left you alone. I should have come to the school or shoved a carrier pigeon down your shirt or learned skywriting or some survivalist shit. I knew it. *Leigh* knew it."

"I was a hostage. You would have lost. You can't negotiate with terrorists."

"I guess." Erin studied the cracks in the wooden table.

"You saved the Rachels for me."

"Leigh did that. We both tried watching, but Leigh got bored after she talked for like twenty minutes straight about primacy."

"Primaries."

"Whatever."

"Erin, I'm afraid it's essential for my mental health for you to become an informed voter," I said.

"Jesus Christ."

"You owe it to yourself and your country."

"Even in the fucking psych ward you are lecturing me. They need to adjust your meds."

I glared at her.

"Too soon? All right. Too soon," she said.

But I laughed in spite of myself.

"All right, I gotta jet. I look forward to putting you back on the schedule. These new girls are just in it for the discount."

"Yes, and I work at Aerie for the love." I rolled my eyes.

"Damn right you do." Erin leaned down and kissed the top of my head. "Later."

I have group therapy in ten minutes. The social worker that runs it kind of looks like Christiane Amanpour. It's good for the recovery process.

Sincerely,

Brynn

Folder: Drafts
To: Brynnieh0401@gmail.com
From: Brynnieh0401@gmail.com
Date: April 11
Subject: A new day

Dear Rachel Maddow,

I'm glad to be out. Every day cost a shit ton of money, and even though Mom has some kick-ass insurance, there was a limit on me being there. Mom stopped by once to tell me that I better not have to come back, or else Fart Weasel would find out. I'm fucked up on my own, I know, but I can't help but thank her stellar parenting for me being partly the way I am. My inpatient team is hooking me up with a social worker and a legal aide and another social worker and oh, what now? Another social worker! There is a lot of social work in my future. Eighteen-year-olds can drop out of school, but being a minor who nearly (ACCIDENTALLY, THANK YOU VERY MUCH) died out of desperation can occasionally net you some support, especially if your mom-who-doesn't-want-you-anymore works at a really good hospital.

That is some fucked-up ironic shit right there.

"I'm still unwell," I said to Erin when she picked me up from the hospital. I could sign myself out, being eighteen and all.

"Point me to the person who's really happy, truly happy," she said.

"Sorry about the beer," I said.

"It's okay. There won't be any more in the house for a long time."

"I won't drink it. It's the worst thing on Earth."

"Do you feel like dying anymore?"

"I never did," I said. "Not really. That wasn't it. I just . . . I was tired. Tired of Adam. Tired of Mom. Tired of being responsible for possibly ruining Michaela's life again. Tired of being tired. I should have just gone to bed. But . . ." I trailed off.

I was still too tired to explain.

So, at Erin's I went to sleep. For hours and hours. I'd wake up, stran-gled with thoughts of Nick or Michaela and some Sarah in there because my mind hates me.

What helped most was reading Lacey's e-mails. And Mr. Grimm's. They cared about me. And so did Leigh and Erin. That was more than a lot of people get.

I wondered if Nick was tired. Is that what he wanted, the night he overdosed? Rest? Peace? A new skin, a new life? I'd never know. Right now, alone and raw in the safety of Erin and Leigh's place, it was too much to think about him. How I almost *did* end up like him. I didn't want that. I want . . . something else.

I'll think of it later. After I sleep.

Sincerely,
Brynn

Folder:	Sent
To:	Rachel@msnbc.com
From:	Brynnieh0401@gmail.com
Date:	April 14
Subject:	RE: Questions

Dear Rachel Maddow,

Hello! Remember me? Queen Overshare? Humor helps me cope!

Part of me hopes you didn't read all of my letters. Part of me is just mortified thinking of the staffer who suffered through any of it.

Although, this means that I *did* technically send you all the answers to Mr. Grimm's questions, relieving myself of the existential guilt carried by having disappointed him in yet another way. He always kept asking if I replied to you from the beginning of the year. That might have made this past year almost worth it. (Almost.) Maybe one day you'll get to meet him. You'd like him. He's sure to save the world at least once and merit a spot on The Interview.

I still write to you (offline, oh my e-mail, OFFLINE). I hope you don't mind. You're like my patronus or at least my Patron Saint of Reporting Stuff That Sucks but Still Encouraging Civic Involvement Anyway.

Thank you again.

Sincerely,

Brynn

Dear Rachel Maddow,

I went back to school today. Not much had changed.

Lacey was happy I was still alive.

So was Mr. Grimm.

Bianca, Riley, Lance, and Greg also seemed pleased.

Happiest of all was Justin. He is thrilled that I'm back on the paper, even if I'm just going to help brainstorm and maybe edit for a bit. (Which is comical. Me. Edit. Maybe Justin can read the articles out loud to me. I can tell him how they sound. Actually, I think the computer does that. Maybe I'll ask.)

Investigative journalist that he is, he had found out who had tried to frame me before the election. And then he had the unhappy task of dropping that truth bomb about Sarah on me.

I stared at him after he told me she had definitely been the one to log in to my fucking school e-mail and send the pictures of Adam from my account. I knew it was a possibility, but I couldn't bring myself to believe it was true until Justin told me.

"Say that again," I said slowly.

Justin repeated the story. The library cameras showed her going into the library. She had logged in as me. Logged in to the e-mail as me. They knew it wasn't me because the time stamp of the e-mails matched the time stamp on the video.

Thanks, surveillance state.

My mouth hung open. It felt like my blood stopped pumping and my lungs stopped expanding.

Justin shifted uncomfortably.

After a moment, I realized that my body hadn't ceased to function because Sarah had actually been the one who tried to seriously fuck me over. Blood pumped. Oxygen entered and exited just as before. Sarah *had* broken my heart, multiple times. But Erin and Leigh and Lacey and Mr. Grimm and some medication and meditation at Mom's excellent hospital had welded those few pieces back together. It wouldn't shatter in the same places again.

The scars still burned, though. I could physically feel her betrayal in my chest. In my entire body. I had loved her and in the end she had only ever loved herself.

Because how else could she have done that?

How?

"How could she have done that?" I asked Justin.

"I can't even imagine," said Justin.

And he had as much of an imagination as I did.

We sat there with our silent, failed imaginations together.

That helped a little.

I'm glad I'm only allowed back half days this week. The thought of staying here, in school, where everything happened . . . it was still too much. Next week I'll be back to full days.

Justin feels we should now spend our time looking in to the materials used to renovate the War Memorial and what role that played in the fire.

I admit I'm intrigued.

But. One day at a time. That's what my counselor says.

I'm not dropping out yet, at least. If I did, I wouldn't get to be on the paper.

Michaela hasn't been back, either. Lacey's aide said she is doing homeschool temporarily. She couldn't find out if Michaela was ever coming back.

Sincerely,

Brynn

Folder:	Drafts
To:	Brynnieh0401@gmail.com
From:	Brynnieh0401@gmail.com
Date:	April 16
Subject:	Filters

Dear Rachel Maddow,

Holy fuckballs. MICHAELA WROTE TO ME AND IT WENT TO SPAM. She might think I'm dead. I should get a new phone. Mom and Fart Weasel never gave me mine back. But I'll be back at Aerie eventually, and can afford my own. Though, her number was stored in the one they took, damn it all.

Folder: Drafts
To: Brynnieh0401@gmail.com
From: Brynnieh0401@gmail.com
Date: May 1
Subject: Filters

Dear Rachel Maddow,

I'm back to work at Aerie. It is strangely therapeutic.

"Erin," I said at the end of the night.

"Mmm," she said, shuffling papers on the desk in the back office.

"If you had to find someone who didn't want to be found, what would you do?" I asked.

Erin looked up. "Huh?" she said.

"I need to find someone. A girl. My girlfriend. Or . . . at least she was."

"Does she go to your school?"

"Yes," I said.

"Then find her at school."

"That has not been successful."

"I doubt you really tried," she said.

She was right, but still.

"Though," Erin said, looking thoughtful. "Don't you have any clever ne'er-do-wells in your life who could help you out with this sort of thing?"

"Ne'er-do-well? Who says that anymore?"

"I do," said Erin.

I thought about that. I did have several such people at my disposal.

In case God creeps on e-mails like a cosmic Homeland Security operative or whatever, I want to put in an application for Erin, Patron Saint of Girls' Underwear and Likely Doomed Love Affairs. She inspired me to action, if nothing else.

It was too late to go tonight. But . . . tomorrow. Watch this space.

Sincerely,

Brynn

Folder: Drafts
To: Brynnieh0401@gmail.com
From: Brynnieh0401@gmail.com
Date: May 2
Subject: All is fair

Dear Rachel Maddow,

Thanks to Lacey's aide, I had in my possession Michaela's home address.

Michaela lives two bus rides and a steep hike away from Leigh and Erin. I looked her address up online over and over just to make sure. I panted my way up the hill, trying to channel the little blue engine who applied or whatever that book is. As I summited the avenue, I muttered internally about mountain dwellers because I didn't have breath to spare to curse out loud.

After I caught my breath, I slogged along the poorly maintained sidewalks until I reached the address saved in my new phone. The house looked . . . normal. Brown tiles. Roof. Windows. Not even a moldering couch or anything on the porch. Just . . . house. I kept walking. When I got a block away and the street started to slope down again, I turned around, crossed the street, and went back. I stared at her house across the asphalt and concrete. Was she even home? Was this legal? This was surely a terrible idea. She hated me. What was I even doing?

This went on for at least a half an hour. Eventually it started to rain so that I had to either shit or get off the pot. So I stepped onto the porch. I went to the door, and before I could think better of it, I rang the bell. A moment passed. And then another one. "Oh, whelp, gotta go, hey, at least I tried . . ." I thought. But then the door swung open. A tiny woman with silver hair wearing a tentlike robe stood in front of me.

"Um. Hello, ma'am," I said. I really should have prepared a script. "I was wondering if Michaela is home?"

The tiny lady's face lit up. "Are you a little friend?" She beamed. "Come to play with Chaela! Oh, how nice."

"Gram, don't stand by the door. It's getting cold," I heard Michaela call from inside.

I don't know if my heart stopped, but it felt like it did. The tiny lady withdrew from the doorway, and I heard her say something. Then Michaela came to the door.

"We don't want any . . ." she started, but froze the instant she saw me.

"I'm-so-sorry-the-whole-thing-was-my-fault-I'm-so-not-into-politics-but-Lacey-you-know-she's-going-to-Penn-so-it's-all-good-but-Rachel-Maddow-is-so-damn-cheerful-maybe-you-don't-watch-her-MSNBC-anyway-I'm-so-so-so-sorry-actually-okay-I-really-am-into-politics-but-not-like-that-and-I-love-you." Everything came out in one breath.

Holy Cable News Networks, I said the L-word to her. If one leg of this journey or another didn't cause me to pass out or die, then I'd have only luck to thank.

But I wasn't even done.

"YOU ARE PERFECT IN EVERY WAY!" I shouted.

She opened her mouth to speak.

"I'M SORRY I RUIN LIVES," I said.

Next time, Rachel, mark my words: teleprompter. Notes on clipboard.

Actually, fuck that. There will be no next time.

"You didn't ruin my life, Brynn." Michaela sighed. "Others beat you to it." She looked at the ground. "*I* beat you to it. Come in. You're freezing."

"Thank you," I said. I stepped inside the house and looked around. It was like a gingerbread home. The couch appeared to be shrink-wrapped in plastic. Every flat surface had a round crocheted thingy on it, with little bright ceramic thingies perched on top.

"Gram loves tchotchkes," Michaela explained. "She calls them her 'whimsies.' "

I was sorely tempted to ask what the fuck tchotchkes were, but I gathered they involved ceramics and yarn.

"Listen, I don't have to stay. I just wanted to tell you I'm sorry. If you hate me, I'll . . ."

I didn't know what.

"I get it. Really. But I'm sorry. And . . ." I trailed off.

Michaela came close to me. "You keep saying you're sorry," she said.

"I am."

"For what?"

"For running for stupid SGA so that Adam went after you to get back at me. For him finding and putting up all that stuff. I'm sorry."

"It wasn't your fault."

"But . . ."

"Brynn, that wasn't your fault. I didn't blame you. Believe me, I blame that asshole Adam for that shit."

"Oh." I looked around quizzically. China dolls from a glass cabinet returned my confused glance. "You left. You didn't come back. I didn't . . ."

"How could I possibly come back? Why would you want to talk to me?"

"How could I not not want to . . . wait, what?" I looked to the china dolls for answers. They didn't know what the hell was going on, either.

"That's what happens. When people see the pictures. They don't want to talk to you, right? They whisper behind your back, sure, but not to your face. Stuff got out of hand at my old school, and I wanted the hell out of there. Ol' Ma and Pa thought that Gram wasn't doing so hot, so they thought that they could kill two birds with one stone. Get me a fresh start, and get Gram a cheap caretaker. My uncle lives nearby. But he works afternoons and nights."

"Oh."

"I couldn't face you." Michaela sank onto what appeared to be a plastic-wrapped couch. "How could I?" She put her face in her hands.

I gingerly sat down on the condom couch next to her. "You're facing me now," I said, more gently than I thought myself capable.

"Yeah, well, you found me," she said.

"Do you hate me?" I asked.

"No."

"Do you want me to go?"

"No."

"Okay." I just sat there. You know, Rachel, things often go better with people the less I speak. Or do anything, really.

"He found that online someplace, I guess," Michaela said finally. "I don't search anymore. Most are gone. But. You know."

I just nodded and eased a little closer to her. Her body relaxed.

"Don't think I'm a victim. Or, maybe I am, even though my shrink doesn't like that word. But I'm not innocent. I *was* with a guy. Well, two guys. And another girl. I dated a lot, but only one person at a time. Well, within a pretty short time. But there was this party, and I got shit-faced. And I don't even remember any of that, any of those pictures. I'm not proud of that. And there was this *other* girl who none of us liked and God knows what happened to her. She pressed charges, over the pictures taken of her. She wanted me to go in with her, but I wouldn't. Even so, it became 'Michaela is a slut,' you know? God, I'm not making any sense. But you can . . . the pictures got online and it went around the school. And that other girl, the one I wouldn't help? I was so mean to her. Brynn, it was fucked up. I fucked up. So I moved here to get a new start and a new shrink, but some things follow you. Forever. And I guess I deserve that."

She stopped talking. She put her face in her hands again, tears streaming down her cheeks.

I just sat there. I tried to wipe her cheek with my sleeve. You know what, Rachel? I probably don't need to feel sorry for myself as much as I do.

Eventually Michaela's breaths evened out. She got up and got tissues to blow her nose. That was good, because apparently I do not dress in particularly absorbent fabric. She sat back down on the condom couch. "You're still here," she said.

"Of course."

"You're not freaked out?"

"No. I mean, that really sucks. A lot."

"Do you think I'm a slut?"

"I . . ." I thought. "No."

"Do you think I'm awful?"

"Of course not. Who am I to judge anybody?" I shrugged. "Listen, I watch a lot of political commentary. And I can tell you people mess up all the time. Like, huge. And most of them aren't even sorry. They are sorry they get caught, maybe. But not sorry for the shit they caused other people."

"Oh," Michaela said. "Believe me, I'm sorry for that."

"Well, then, there you go. You are more righteous than a good portion of our elected leaders." I nodded again at her. Putting this in political terms calmed me. "All we can do is try to do better. And if you still like the sex with the ladies and the mens? Well? Again. Who am I to say? Thank you, Space Jesus. Amen."

"What's with the Space Jesus? You say that sometimes." A faint smile played at her lips.

"He's the only son of Space God," I said.

"You're ridiculous." Michaela sniffle-laughed again.

"Yes."

"But you're here."

"Also true."

"Okay."

"Okay," I said. "Sooo . . . are we good?"

"Yeah. I guess," she sighed.

"Listen. I'm done with politics forever. My life is in reporting things. Explaining the news to people. Like Lacey tells me, you should just own your shit and keep your head up."

"Seriously?" she said. "That's Lacey's life advice?"

"One hundred percent."

"That sounds . . ." Her smile was real now. "Reasonable."

"Lacey actually asked about you," I said.

"Oh, Lacey," she said.

"Yeah. I failed her. And the blue room. Adam won."

"Well, at least you tried," she said.

"I could live my life by those words. Put them on my tombstone. 'Here lies Brynn. At least she tried.' "

At that moment, Michaela's grandmother emerged from a doorway at the back of the house. "Chaela, baby! It is time for your nap! Your little friend should run home now." She looked at me. "Bet you need a nap, too, sweetie!"

"That is not a bad idea, ma'am," I said.

"What a good girl." She nodded approvingly at me.

"Bye, Brynnie," said Michaela, pulling me off the couch and kind of shoving me toward the door. "She gets weird quick. Get out while you can," she whispered. "I'll see you on Monday."

"Okay. Bye!" I called.

"What a good girl," I heard from inside.

I walked down the hill, which wasn't much more fun than going up the hill, but at least I could breathe.

Technically I professed my love to Michaela and she didn't throw up. So I have another best new thing in the world. She could change her mind and throw up tomorrow, maybe. But she didn't today. Sometimes you have to rejoice in what you can in this life.

Sincerely,

Brynn

Folder: Drafts
To: Brynnieh0401@gmail.com
From: Brynnieh0401@gmail.com
Date: May 3
Subject: And better yet

Dear Rachel Maddow,

Michaela wrote her number down for me again when I visited. I texted to let her know my new number.

She texted back. "I love you, too."

I am still tired. But maybe I'll try to stay awake a little more tomorrow. Just to read those words over, and over, and over.

Sincerely,

Brynn

Folder:	Drafts
To:	Brynnieh0401@gmail.com
From:	Brynnieh0401@gmail.com
Date:	May 4
Subject:	Speaking of over

Dear Rachel Maddow,

I was feeling pretty good when I left. Until I walked out of the mall and saw Sarah sitting on the bench outside.

I stopped.

I remembered to breathe. I tried to remember what they taught me in the hospital. Take a breath. Then another.

I started to walk again. I had to get away from her as quickly as possible.

"Brynn, wait, please," she said.

I didn't have to listen. I owed her nothing, after what she tried to pull. But I stopped.

"I'm sorry," Sarah said. "I really am. I know you must hate me. It's just that Adam was so awful. And we were broken up, so we couldn't fight him together. And I didn't think. . . ."

"Oh, you thought," I said. "You thought about what was good for *you*. In the end, that's always what you do. I wasn't worth keeping around. So it was 'bye-bye, Brynn. Who cares what happens to her? She's a fuckup anyway.'"

Tears welled in her eyes. "No, I swear, I didn't mean for you to get hurt."

I held up my hands. The fragile new skin knitting the pieces of me together strained with her every word.

"Good-bye, Sarah." I turned and willed my feet to take me away from her. She said something else, but I tuned her out.

Everything hurt near her. But it hurt a little less the farther away I got.

Someday, maybe it wouldn't hurt at all.

I'd just have to keep breathing until then.

Sincerely,

Brynn

Folder: Sent
To: Brynnieh0401@gmail.com
From: mmaynard@westing.pa.edu
Date: May 9
Subject: RE:

Dear Ms. Harper,

After exhausting all possible avenues of information, we have come to the conclusion that you were in no way involved with harassing Adam Graff or any other student at Westing High. I know this semester, and this incident in particular, has caused you a great deal of stress. I offer my deepest apologies. Also, if I can do anything to help you during the rest of your time at Westing High, please don't hesitate to reach out.

Sincerely,

Principal Mark Maynard

Folder: Sent
To: Rachel@msnbc.com
From: Brynnieh0401@gmail.com
Date: September 10
Subject: (Postscript

Dear Rachel Maddow,

We are so close to the next presidential election cycle. I imagine you sleep even less now than you do usually. It works out for me, because you are on TV way more often.

I tried to get Michaela to come over to Leigh and Erin's to watch you. She claimed to have too much homework. She said she might only consider it if it were Chris Hayes.

The heart wants what it wants, I guess.

Justin is busy running things as a fair and just SGA president. (He listened to the will of the people and is trying a pilot program with a local farm to get green peas. The ketchup shortage remains a work in progress.) Michaela (who came back this fall) convinced me to go to summer school to improve my GPA even more. With all of that academic achievement (2.5!), I am back at the school paper with everyone's blessing. Adam is gone, so we have all of the fancy new equipment, but none of the censorship. Sarah is gone, too; her parents pulled her out for online homeschool. I saw her one more time before she left. We didn't even speak. She just broke down crying. She just broke down, period.

I hope Sarah comes out of that all right, even if I never want to see her again. I really do. I know what it feels like, to be that low.

As it turned out, the school board superintendent committee seat opened up again once Adam no longer was around to fill it. Since the paper is the only thing I ever really cared about, there didn't even need to be another runoff. Bianca ended up expressing her interest in the spot. It turns out she found everything inspiring. Since no one else wanted it, it became hers. She's really into finding the right person to represent everyone's interests.

Lacey is settled into Penn like a boss. Justin swoons like a diva, dramatically declaring he misses her most at least once a day. But that cannot possibly be true. Lacey is my heart. But my heart is off killing it Ivy-style, which keeps me going on the bad days.

Given what Ms. Yee just taught about chaos theory (and, oh, do I contribute to chaos), I'd like to think that maybe *my* shot at politics will one day contribute to the next female presidential candidate a little, itty-bitty bit. Like, if a viceroy butterfly flaps its wings in northern Mexico and that makes a storm that waters the crops in Maine, surely my bid for a seat of power at Westing High might somehow contribute to electing the first woman president. Though sure, another megalomaniacal solipsistic narcissistic dude bro might win against her. But I'd like to think he wouldn't. And even if he did, there will be people like you to call him out.

And maybe, in some little, itty-bitty way—people like me.

Thank you again, Rachel, for your optimism and passion. Even if you don't always feel it, you demonstrate it. And that's been enough to keep me going.

Civic engagement is mostly just talking and listening to the people, Mr. Grimm says.

You kick ass at that every day.

So I will try to kick ass, too.

Your fan always,
Brynn

Acknowledgments

This book would be dedicated to my mother, but she did not approve of all the swearing. So I will instead thank her here for her lifelong love, support, and candid editorial comments.

I have also been blessed with so many family and friends who have supported me along the way. I've been writing for as long as I can remember, and as such have been forcing my writing on people just as long. I don't want to miss anyone in print, but know that I cherish you. Thank you all.

Thank you to Catherine Drayton, agent extraordinaire, who was the first one to take a chance on a strange epistolary YA written to a real person. I try to be the best writer I can if only to impress you. Thanks also to the Inkwell team, all of whom I am glad to have in my corner.

Anna Roberto is a stone-cold genius of an editor and someone with whom I wish I could hang out every day. I am forever grateful to her and to the entire Feiwel & Friends team for their brilliance and expertise.

The VCFA Writing for Children and Young Adults MFA is the best decision I ever made. The faculty, particularly Na An, Amanda Jenkins, Daniel José Older, and Amy King picked me up, brushed me off, and gifted me their boundless knowledge and kind spirits. Thank you to them, the students and alumni, and to my beloved Dead Post-its Society for a powerful community that keeps me writing.

Thank you to the many other teachers I've had through the years, particularly those at Albright College and Boston University. Dr. William King, the Rev. Paul Clark, Dr. Bryan Stone, Dr. Claire Wolfteich, and Dr. Donna Freitas let me write creatively and about children's literature to my heart's content. I don't know that I could come up with an exhaustive list of every great teacher I've had (Ms. McClain! Ms. Lech! Dr. Shirk! Dr. Pankratz! Dr. de Syon! Sra. Ozment! Dra. Meléndez! Dr. Huck! Dr. Warfield!), because looking back I spent an awful lot of time in school. But thanks to everyone who had the misfortune to educate me. I appreciate every last one of you.

I want to send a special shout-out to Josh Groban. Because I wrote a book and am mad with the power to put anything I want in print. *Closer* will always be my favorite album, Josh, in case you needed to know.

Thank you to all of my colleagues and students at Wheelock College. I have such great love and respect for you lot. Even if Wheelock won't exist as such by the time this book comes out, know that it only ever really existed in all of you. Your passion, your drive, and your tremendous heart are its legacy that will abide. I am so, so grateful I got to be a part of your journey.

Finally, thank you to Peter, Katherine, and Charles, who make it nearly impossible to complete novels. I love you anyway.